The
BRONZE
CAULDRON

Geraldine McCaughrean

MYTHS and LEGENDS of the WORLD

THE BRONZE CAULDRON

Illustrated by
Bee Willey

Orion
Children's Books

By the same author and illustrator

MYTHS AND LEGENDS OF THE WORLD
THE GOLDEN HOARD
THE SILVER TREASURE

FOR AILSA
If I could I would give you all the stories in the world
G.M.

FOR JUDITH
With big thank yous
B.W.

First published in Great Britain in 1997
by Orion Children's Books
a division of the Orion Publishing Group Ltd
Orion House
5 Upper St Martin's Lane
London WC2H 9EA

Text copyright © Geraldine McCaughrean 1997
Illustrations copyright © Bee Willey 1997
Designed by Dalia Hartman

A catalogue record for this book is available from the British Library.

Printed in Italy

ISBN 1 85881 275 5

Contents

Dragons to Dine

A HITTITE MYTH

TARU TOOK his lightning in one hand and his thunderbolt in the other and went out to fight the dragon Illuyankas. From Aleppo to Kayseri it lay, a mountain range of a monster, armoured with scales as large as oven doors, and green as the mould that grows on graves.

Behind it lay the ruins of cities, fallen forests, plains cracked like dinner plates, lakes drunk dry. One yellow eye surveyed the devastation done, the other looked ahead to lands as yet untouched. That eye came to rest on Taru, god of wind and weather, armed for battle and calling its name.

"Illuyankas! Illuyankas! Stand and fight! You have cracked open this world like an egg and chewed to pieces everything Mankind has made. But you shall not take one step more! All the weather of the world is in my quiver, and the gods have sent me to stop you where you stand!"

Illuyankas yawned gigantically, and licked the moon with a rasping tongue. When Taru mustered the clouds and blew them over the dragon's back, drenching it in rain, the rainwater evaporated in clouds of steam. When blizzards enfolded the beast in driving snow and sleet, the icy droplets simply cascaded off it in torrents of meltwater. Taru tore shreds off the north wind and, shaping them in his hands, pelted the dragon's head. But Illuyankas, though it rocked back on its heels, only snapped its jaws shut around the missiles and cracked them between its bronze teeth.

For a time, Taru drew back his wild weather and let the sun scorch the dragon's back. But Illuyankas's hide, like a roof of glass, reflected the sunlight, and it rebounded on Taru, dazzling him and wilting the lightning in his hand.

Tara pounded on the dragon with thunder. He whipped it with whirlwinds. But after a day, Illuyankas merely flicked its tremendous tail and flung Taru seven miles into the sky before continuing to graze on the people and villages of the Earth. Lifting its snout and flaring its nostrils, it let out a beacon of fire and a roaring whistle - a summons - and from below the earth, out through the craters of volcanoes everywhere, came smaller, squirming dragons, the children of Illuyankas.

They feared nothing from the paltry people scurrying like ants between their claws. For not even the people's gods could stand in the way of Illuyankas and its kin. Leaping and careering in a boisterous, playful trail of destruction, the great green family came to the palace of the goddess Inaras. That was where, for the first time, they saw a smiling face. It startled them to a standstill.

"Welcome! Welcome, glorious creatures!" cried Inaras, spreading her arms in a gesture of hospitality and gladness. "Won't you rest and eat? See! I've prepared a meal for you. If you are going to rule the world from now on, you must be honoured as kings are honoured and feasted like emperors."

Laid out on the ground in front of the palace were white cloths a mile long, strewn with dishes of gold. In the dishes was food of every kind - fish baked and fried, vegetables raw and cooked, meat roasted and rare.

There were barrels of wine and casks of beer, sherbets and curds and cheeses. There were cakes and loaves, baskets of nuts and tureens of caramel sugar. Honey-soaked haavala was heaped as high as haystacks.

The dragons browsed at first, taking a lick here, a taste there. But soon they were gorging frenziedly, so delicious were the offerings Inaras laid before them. All day and all night and for three more days and nights the dragons dined, and Inaras never slept, so intent was she on bringing them more food, more drink, more deliciousness.

The dragons began to feel sleepy, and stumbling a little against the pink palace walls, they turned for home. Their bellies were so bloated, their eyes so heavy that it was all they could do to find the individual entrances to their underground lairs. Belching and hiccuping, the baby dragons rolled into their volcanic craters and thrust their heads into the tunnels from which they had emerged. *Oof.* Neck and shoulders passed inside. *Oooff.* Their stomachs did not.

So fat were Illuyankas and the lesser dragons that they could not manage to climb back through their doors. They could not reach their warm nests, their lava troughs, the vats of molten rock at which they drank to recharge their dragonish fire. And when they tried, they could not back out again, either. It was Inaras's turn to light beacons and to whistle. Out from the ruins of their villages, out from the rubble of cities and farms and the fallen forests came all the little people of the Earth, carrying enough new rope to bind the moon to the sun.

They ran to where the dragons stood, heads underground, stomachs and hind-quarters in the sun, writhing and tugging to free themselves. The people bound the dragons and hog-tied them, roped them, knee and ankle, and peeled off their scales, leaving the dragons pink and vulnerable, naked and sunburned.

"Thank you, Taru, for your fierceness and bravery!" they sang. "But thank you, Inaras, even more, for your cunning and your cooking!"

Inaras inclined her head graciously and invited the people to finish up the crumbs of the dragons' feast. And Taru (when he came back down from the sky) held off bad weather until the people had had time to mend their roofs.

The Bronze Cauldron

A WELSH LEGEND

THREE PACES from the door, three paces from the window, three paces from where Boy Gwion slept on the floor, stood the witch's bronze cauldron on three bronze legs. It was always bubbling, always steaming, filling the room with horrible smells. Boy Gwion had to gather twigs to feed the fire under it. He had to weed the garden, feed the dogs, sweep the floor, bake the bread, and wash the clothes - though the Old White Sow never changed hers. No one dared come near the witch's house, so Boy's life was lonely. But he was not one to complain.

In the next room, Afagddu the witch's son slept in a white bed and never went hungry. But Boy would not have changed places with Afagddu. His face was as ugly as a dish of eels, and the rest of him all clenched up like a fist. He was the reason why the Old White Sow came and went, to

5

and fro, day and night, feeding the great bronze cauldron.

She brought things soft and hard, blue things and red, nameless things and things too horrible to name. Sometimes she took a ladle and poured a drop of the brew down Afagddu's throat. But he only gaped back at her like a cuckoo chick, his two eyes dull as mud. "Not yet, not yet," crooned the Old White Sow kissing his scurvy head, "but one day soon, my darling, I shall give you better than beauty."

Seven times each day she kicked Boy Gwion. "Don't you ever go stealing that broth, brat. The day you do is the day you die."

Boy nodded. He was always hungry, but not so hungry that he wanted to taste the horrible slop in the bronze cauldron.

At all hours of day and night the witch's hooves scuffed the floor as she brought things from the forest and things from the pond, things from the hedgerow and things from the drain; dry things and wet things, cold things and hot. She fed that cauldron till its brew bubbled treacly, close to the brim. "Stir it and don't stop," she told Boy, "But not a taste, not a lick, for the day you do is the day you die."

Boy shrugged. He had no wish in the world to taste the brew in the cauldron..

One night the Old White Sow was merrier than usual. "Nearly there, nearly there," she crooned to Afagddu, as she tucked him into bed. "Soon now, I know it!" She put on her cloak and took down her basket from the roofbeam. "Stir, brat! Stir!" she told Boy, and with one more kick, scuffled out into the dark.

Boy stirred with one hand and held his nose with the other, while next door Afagddu snored. The seething bubbles brought nasty, shapeless things to the surface which sank again with a sigh. There were glittering shapes, too, and threads of scarlet. The cauldron spoon was as long as a broom, but Boy went on stirring and stirring all night.

Just before dawn, a rising bubble burst, and three drops spurted on to Boy Gwion's hand.

"Ow!"

He rammed his thumb into his mouth to ease the pain. The three drops left three tastes on his tongue: sweet, salt and sour. Then, into Boy's head burst three stars, and he reeled and staggered and fell.

He saw hill-forts and earthworks, stone circles and bonfires.

He saw the King, the butcher, the beggar and the maid.

He saw machines that could fly, buildings sky-high and mines as deep as hell; saw guns and geysers of oil.

He saw how and why and when and where and who, and all in the space of his brainpan, like magnesium burning.

He saw the past and how, long ago, the witch had stolen him from his cradle. He saw the present and how, that very moment, she was coming up the path. He saw the future and how she would kill him for what he

7

had done. All time was inside him, as well as words in millions - as many as the stars - all waiting to be said.

The Old White Sow pushed open the door with a grunt. She saw at once what had happened. "Wretch! Rascal! Robber! That was for Afagddu! That was for my boy!" She snatched up the ladle and carried a slopping scoop through to her son, splashing it, hot, into his open mouth. But all the liquor's magic had been in those three drops that burned Boy's thumb. The moment of perfection was past, and Afagddu would have no genius to make up for his ugliness.

Before the witch came back from the bedroom, Boy Gwion fled through the open door. He had glimpsed the mysteries of magic now, and he knew how to change his shape. So he ran his hands through his hair, until his hair turned to ears; he stretched out his body and ran . . . into the shape of a hare.

The Old White Sow came after him, turning herself into a greyhound, the better to catch him.

"Stop and stay, thief," she barked, "for if you've seen the future, you know that I shall kill you!" Her lean and bony body gained on the hare, jaws agape and tongue lolling. A river lay in their path. Boy was trapped.

Feeling hot breath on his back, Hare Gwion read magic words off the inside of his eyelids and, speaking them aloud, turned himself into a fish. *Plop*, the squealing hare splashed into the water - a glitter of scales, a flutter of fins - and swam away. The greyhound tumbled in behind.

But as she sank, the Old White Sow turned herself into an otter. A lithe

writhe of sleek brown fur sped through after the fish, claws ripping the water to foam. The fish flickered through a streaming forest of weed; his dappled back almost invisible over the mottled riverbed. But the otter only came on, with ravenous jaws.

"Stop and stay, villain, for if you've seen the future, you know I shall eat you!"

In his terror, Fish Gwion leapt clear out of the water, and hearing magic words pound in his ears, he spoke them aloud – and turned into a bird. Steep as a lark he soared into the sky. But the Old White Sow only shook the water off her back and turned herself into a hawk. High as the treetops, high as the hilltops, high as an arrow can be shot, flew Bird Gwion. But between him and the sun, casting a cold shadow over him, stooped the hawk-witch, talons spread.

"Stay and die, filcher," she shrieked, "for if you have seen the future, you know that I shall swallow you down!"

Down.

Down swooped Bird Gwion, in at the gaping door of a barn, down on to the threshing floor where harvested ears of corn lay waiting to be threshed. Every ear held a hundred grains, and each grain exactly like every other. Feeling his heart thud out magic words, Bird Gwion spoke them aloud and . . . changed himself into a grain of corn: one grain among a million.

But grain cannot run.

Bck-bck-bck.

The witch turned herself into a chicken and came strutting into the barn. She pecked from morning till night. Scratch-peck. Scratch-peck. "Lie there and die, Grain Gwion, for if you have seen the future, you know I shall . . . *bck-bck-bck.*"

The grain that was Boy Gwion went down the chicken's throat. She stretched up her head and crowed in triumph, then shook off her feathers and went home to where the cauldron stood cold and congealing.

Did you know, did you know, that grains grow in the dark?

Nine months later, the Old White Sow put a hand to her great belly and gave a scream, like a chicken before its neck is wrung.

"Is there no ridding the world of that thieving Boy?"

She gave birth to a child so beautiful that his forehead shone like bronze and his small hands plucked music from the witch's lank hair.

His brightness hurt the witch's eyes. She bundled her baby into a sack and slung it over her shoulder. "Wretch! Thief! Slave! I will not love you! I shall not love you! Let no one say I ever gave you life!" Then she went to the river, where, as an otter, she had chased Fish Gwion, and she flung her baby into the water to die.

Currents caught the sack, eddies spun it, and the undertow dragged it down into dark, drowning depths. It rolled over the stones where the salmon spawn, it washed over the weir where the salmon fishermen fish. And there the sack was found by the King's own fisherman, wound three times round with golden fishline.

They called the baby Taliesin, which means "bright brow"; a child so handsome that the King prized him in the way he prized the work of his goldsmiths. But only when Taliesin opened his mouth did the King realize what riches had come to him in a hessian sack. For Taliesin the poet spoke of the past, present and future, of how, why, when, where, and who. And when he sang songs, to the music of the King's harpist, he had at his beck words in millions, as many as the stars and twice as bright.

Guitar Solo

A MYTH FROM MALI

IN A PLACE where six rivers join like the strings of a guitar, lived Zin the Nasty, Zin the mean, Zin-Kibaru the water spirit. Even above the noise of rushing water rose the sound of his magic guitar, and whenever he played it, the creatures of the river fell under his power. He summoned them to dance for him and to fetch him food and drink. In the daytime, the countryside rocked to the sound of Zin's partying.

But come night-time, there was worse in store for Zin's neighbour, Faran. At night, Zin played his guitar in Faran's field, hidden by darkness and the tall plants. Faran was not rich. In all the world he only had a field, a fishing-rod, a canoe and his mother. So when Zin began to play, Faran clapped his hands to his head and groaned, "Oh no! Not again!"

Out of the rivers came a million mesmerized fish, slithering up the bank, walking on their tails, glimmering silver. They trampled his green shoots, gobbled his tall leaves, picked his ripe crop to carry home to Zin-Kibaru. Like a flock of crows they stripped his field, and no amount of shoo-ing would drive them away. Not while Zin played his spiteful, magic guitar.

"We shall starve!" complained Faran to his mother.

"Well, boy," she said, "there's a saying I seem to recall: when the fish eat your food, it's time to eat the fish."

So Faran took his rod and his canoe and went fishing. All day he fished, but Zin's magic simply kept the fish away, and Faran caught nothing. All night he fished, too, and never a bite: the fish were too busy eating the maize in his field.

"Nothing, nothing, nothing," said Faran in disgust, as he arrived home with his rod over his shoulder.

"Nothing?" said his mother seeing the bulging fishing-basket.

"Well, nothing but two hippopotami," said Faran, "and we can't eat them, so I'd better let them go."

The hippopotami got out of Faran's basket and trotted away. And Faran went to Riversmeet and grabbed Zin-Kibaru by the shirt. "I'll fight you for that guitar of yours!"

Now Zin was an ugly brute, and got most of his fun from tormenting Faran and the animals. But he also loved to wrestle. "I'll fight you, boy," he said, "and if you win, you get my guitar. But if *I* win, I get your canoe. Agreed?"

"If I don't stop your magic, I shan't need no canoe," said Faran, " 'cos I'll be starved right down to a skeleton, me and Mama both."

So, that was one night the magic guitar did not play in Faran's field – because Faran and Zin were wrestling.

All the animals watched. At first they cheered Zin: he had told them to. But soon they fell silent, a circle of glittering eyes.

All night Faran fought, because so much depended on it. "Can't lose my canoe!" he thought, each time he grew tired. "Must stop that music!" he thought, each time he hit the ground. "Must win, for Mama's sake!" he thought, each time Zin bit or kicked or scratched him.

And by morning it really seemed as if Faran might win.

"Come on, Faran!" whispered a monkey and a duck.

"COME ON, FARAN!" roared his mother.

Then Zin cheated.

He used a magic word.

"Zongballyboshbuckericket!" he said, and Faran fell to the ground like spilled water. He could not move. Zin danced round him, hands clasped above his head - "I win! I win! I win!" - then laughed and laughed till he had to sit down.

"Oh Mama!" sobbed Faran. "I'm sorry! I did my best, but I don't know no magic words to knock this bully down!"

"Oh yes you do!" called his mama. "Don't you recall? You found them in your fishing basket one day!"

Then Faran remembered. The perfect magic words. And he used them.

"Hippopotami! HELP!"

Just like magic, the first hippopotamus Faran had caught came and sat down - just where Zin was sitting. I mean *right on the spot* where Zin was sitting. And then his hippopotamus mate came and sat on his lap. And that, it was generally agreed, was when Faran won the fight.

So nowadays Faran floats half-asleep in his canoe, fishing or playing a small guitar. He has changed the strings, of course, so as to have no magic power over the creatures of the six rivers. But he does have plenty of friends to help him tend his maize and mend his roof and dance with his mother. And what more can a boy ask than that?

Sadko and the Tsar of the Sea

A RUSSIAN LEGEND

THERE WAS a time when Russia was peopled with heroes, and every day brought adventure. All the deeds were great and worth the doing, and all the cargoes were king's ransoms. Even so, these heroes - the *bogatyri* - were not the greatest powers on Earth, and they were still bound by laws and etiquette and taxes. So when Sadko the Merchant set sail with a cargo of gems, he *ought* to have paid tribute to the Tsar of the Sea.

Suddenly, with a jolt which spilled sackloads of rubies along the deck, the ship stopped moving. The wind tugged at the sail, waves spilled over the stern, but the ship stood as still as if it were rooted to the seabed. The crew looked over the side, but there was no sandbar, no reef. A terrible realization dawned on Sadko.

"The Tsar of the Sea wants his toll!" he exclaimed. "Fetch it! Pay it!

Fetch twice the amount! How could I have been so forgetful, so lacking in respect?" Scooping up a handful of pearls, another of emeralds and two of diamonds, he spread them on a plank of wood and, leaning over the side, set the gems afloat.

"More sail and on!" cried the captain, but the ship stayed stuck fast, like an axehead sunk in a log.

Sadko smote his forehead, tore his coat and leapt on to the ship's rail. "It's no good! The Tsar is affronted! My offence was too great! He requires a life, and a life he shall have!" So saying, he fell face-first on to the plank, scattering pearls and soaking the fur collar of his coat. "Take me!" he cried (for this *was* the Age of Heroes).

Nothing happened except that the plank floated away from the ship, the ship from the plank. The captain sailed on without a backward glance, and Sadko lay face-down on the sea, wondering about sharks. The ocean rocked him, the sun shone on his back. Sadko fell asleep.

So he never did know how he came to wake in the palace of the Tsar of the Sea. Its ceiling was silvered with mother-of-pearl, its vaulting the ribs of a hundred whales. Conch-shell fanfares blew from towers of scarlet coral, and where banners might have flown, shoals of brightly coloured fish unfurled in iridescent thousands. Seated on a giant clam shell, among the gilded figureheads of shipwrecks, sat the Tsar of the Sea, half-man, half-fish, a great green tail coiled around the base of his throne.

"Your tribute, my lord . . ." began Sadko, flinging himself on his face and sliding along the smooth-scaled floor.

"Think nothing of it," said the Tsar graciously. "I had heard of you. I wanted to meet you. This to-ing and fro-ing over the ocean was your idea, I hear."

"It shall stop and never be thought of again!" offered Sadko.

"Not a bit. I like it. Good idea," responded the Tsar, his walrus moustaches flowing luxuriantly about his ears. "It shall be a thing of the future, believe me. D'you play that?" He pointed a fluke of his tail at the balalaika which had fallen from inside Sadko's coat and was floating slowly upwards and out of reach.

Sadko made a porpoise-like leap to retrieve the musical instrument and began casually to pluck its strings. He claimed modestly to have no skill, no musical talent, nothing worthy of the Tsar's hearing. But he played, all the same, and the Tsar's green face lit up with pleasure. He began to thresh his great tail and then to dance, undulating gently at first like a ray, then tossing aside his turtleshell crown and somersaulting about the palace. The goblets were swept off the tables by the backwash. The hangings billowed, rattling their curtain rings.

Naturally, the courtiers followed suit, plunging and gliding, the narwhal beating time with its twisted horn. But none danced as energetically as the Tsar, hair awash, barbules streaming, as he tumbled over and over, spinning and whistling.

High above, on the surface of the sea, waves as high and white as sail-sheets travelled over the water and fell on ships, shrouding them in spray. Lighthouses tumbled like sandcastles, cliffs were gouged hollow by breaking surf. A storm the like of which the seas had never seen raged from the Tropic of Capricorn to the Tropic of Cancer, because the Tsar of the Sea was dancing to Sadko's balalaika. Sadko's ship and twenty more besides came sailing down, drowned sailors caught in their rigging, spilling cargoes on the tide.

Seeing his mistake, Sadko tried to stop, but the Tsar only roared delightedly, "More! More music! I'm happy! I feel like dancing!" So Sadko played on and on, in bright, major keys suited to the Tsar's cheerful mood. At last, with a tug that cut his fingers to the bone, Sadko pretended accidentally to break all the strings of his balalaika, and the music twanged to a halt. "I regret . . . my instrument . . . not another note . . ." he apologized.

"No matter. I was getting tired anyway," panted the Tsar, throwing himself down on a coral couch. "My chariot will take you home." Sadko was conveyed in a shell chariot drawn by salmon, out of the palace caves, in from the ocean and up a saltwater river to its freshwater source.

The experience had so shaken him that, for a long while, he did not set foot on a ship, but made all his journeys overland. Near where the Tsar's chariot had set him down, he built a warehouse where other merchants

could store their goods. It was a novel idea no one had ever had before. But the spot was far from his native city of Novgorod, and he did wish to see his home again before (as was the fate of *bogatyri*) he turned to stone, a boulder in the landscape of history.

Apprehensively, he went to the banks of the River Volga with a plate of salted bread and fed it to the river. "Oh River, will you carry me home to the city of my birth, now that we have dined together?"

The fish ate the bread, but it was the river which thanked him. "You, Sadko, are a man who knows the worth of water."

"Of course! No man can live in it, no man can live without it," said Sadko, and the Volga gurgled with pleasure.

"I must tell my brother that one! 'No man can live in it, no man can ...' Very good! On second thoughts, why don't you tell him yourself? Share some of your excellent bread with my brother, Lake Ilmen, and see how he rewards your generosity."

So Sadko threw salted bread on to the waters of Lake Ilmen, and though the fish ate the bread, it was the lake which thanked him. "You, Sadko, are a man of the future," said Lake Ilmen in his whispering, reedy voice. "May I suggest you cast three fishing nets over me, for I have a present for you from my great grandfather, the Tsar of the Sea."

Sadko cast the three nets, and to his astonishment and the amazement of everyone who helped him that afternoon, the nets filled with all manner of *salt sea* fish - cod and bass, sturgeon and wrasse - and silver salmon, too, though it was not the season, not the season at all! There were so many fish and it was so late in the day that the catch needed to be stored overnight. Sadko's warehouse was the very place.

But in the course of the night, a subtle change overtook the fish in Sadko's warehouse. By morning, when the doors were opened, there was no smell, no smell at all. And all the fish - stacked high as the rafters of Sadko's warehouse - had turned to ingots of solid silver.

In a way, the end began that day. For afterwards, the *bogatyri* of Russia stopped adventuring and doing great deeds. They took to trade: buying and selling, transport and distribution, marketing and striking deals. They made millions of roubles, and their warehouses reached almost to the sky.

But their wealth fired the envy of foreigners, and Russia was invaded by brutish, bad-mannered barbarians. The *bogatyri* fled - or withdrew, perhaps, to discuss economic sanctions. While they debated, they turned, one by one, to stone - boulders in the landscape of history. Were it not for the rivers babbling about them, the lakes whispering their stories, the sea roaring out their names, we would hardly know they had ever existed.

Cupid and Psyche

A ROMAN MYTH

HOW COULD anyone be more beautiful than the goddess of love? Unthinkable, or so Venus thought. But then thought was not her greatest strength. She was all passion, all instinct, all rash impulse and emotion. There is a cool, deep stillness in a thoughtful woman, which attracts like a deep lake on a hot day. Perhaps that is why mortal Psyche's quiet, pensive beauty was so appealing. Some said she was even more beautiful than Venus, the goddess of love.

"Kill her!" Venus told her son. "Chain the wretch to a rock and let's see how lovely she is after Typhon has chewed on her!"

Venus's son, Cupid, was accustomed to being sent on errands by his mother. Armed with his bow and quiver of golden arrows, he would lie in ambush, on her behalf, and fire into the heart of man or woman an arrow tipped with the poison of love. But to wound someone with love was one thing: chaining them to a rock to feed a sea monster was different. Cupid went about his task with horror and disgust. Psyche struggled and pleaded with him. "Who told you to do this? Who hates me this much?" The golden arrows were spilled across the barnacled rock, and Cupid scratched himself in gathering them up. But obedient to his mother, Cupid overpowered the girl and left her there, silently weeping. The sea writhed in blue-green coils around the bare rock.

Typhon smelled the small, sweet, subtle smell of Psyche and started up from the deep-sea trench. Its back and wings were black-feathered like the cormorant, its bulk so great that the ocean churned up its sandy bed, and undersea volcanoes erupted. Jaws agape, Typhon came for its puny meal. Fishy breath blasted the trees on shore, and Psyche, pale as snow, closed her eyes.

Suddenly she felt a new wind, fresher and sweeter. The chains around her turned to flowers, and the rock beneath her feet was suddenly a distant speck on a blue mirror. Zephyrus the Breeze had lifted Psyche and was flying with her through the sky. He carried her to a palace where the sound of the sea whispered everlastingly through whorled walls of shining shell.

Zephyrus himself had no shape. So whose were the steps that echoed each night through the seashell palace? Psyche feared them at first, feared she had been abducted by some monster or collector of pretty women. But when, after several days, she had seen no one, she became easier in her mind, and settled to thinking, which made her happy. So did the flowers which she found every day outside her door.

Then one night, the echoing footsteps came to the side of her bed and out of the darkness a voice said, "It was I who rescued you from the rock, Psyche. I love you, and I want you for my wife. But you must never see me, never see my face."

"Are you Zephyrus?" she asked.

"He only brought you here to my palace. Don't ask my name. Don't try to see my face, or we shall be lost to each other."

Psyche thought for a moment. "I never cared about anything but the beauty of a person's mind and soul," she said. "If in a while I find you are as kind and gentle as you seem, I shall be your wife and never wish for the sun to shine on us both."

Psyche and her mysterious lover knew nothing but happiness within the seashell palace. For a time, Psyche barely thought about anyone else, anywhere else. But she knew that her parents must think her dead, eaten by the sea monster. So one day she asked to be allowed to visit them, to set their minds at rest. Her lover did not want her to go, feared her going, but he did not try to keep her a prisoner. "You may go," he said. "Only promise me you will pay no attention to your sisters if they try to turn you against me."

Zephyrus kindly carried Psyche home to her father's house, where the family were overjoyed to see her alive – oh, so much more than alive! By the time she had finished describing her life at the seashell palace, her sisters were sea-green with envy. "Free to do as you like all day? Showered with presents? He must be really hideous, that lover of yours, or he could have had *anyone!* You should take a look – just one peep – see what an ogre you've won for yourself. Why don't you?" But when they looked up, Psyche had gone, gone with the wind.

Still, Psyche was a thinker, a ponderer and puzzler over riddles. Her fingers told her that her mysterious lover was not furred or scaley, warty, feathered or clawed. His face was smooth between her hands. He felt like a perfect young man. So why must she never see him? Every day her curiosity grew until, at last, she could bear the mystery no longer. So when he was asleep, deep asleep, his breathing slow and steady, she crept to the lamp and lit it, carried the lamp to the bedside and let its gentle light fall on his face. *"You!"*

Oozing from the lamp like great tears, three fat drops of oil fell on to the chest of the sleeping man. His lids lifted; the pupils of his eyes contracted; his mouth opened to reproach her. "What have you done?" Then he was gone.

Gone, too, were the seashell palace, the bed, the flowers, the lamp. They melted away. Psyche found herself on the dark surface of the cold world, all alone. Her foolishness had returned her to the very rock where she had awaited death.

Once again Typhon scented the small, sweet smell of Psyche, but she was too impatient to wait for death in Typhon's jaws. In her despair, she threw herself into the seething sea.

"Oh no!" said the wave. "I will not drown you!"

"Live, Psyche!" said the saltwater. "I will not kill you."

"Go, Psyche!" said the sea. "Your death would stain me black with shame. You must find some other way to die!" And an arching wave flung her ashore.

Refused permission to die, Psyche resolved to live. She turned her wet face towards the rainy sky. "I shall never rest till I've found you!" she shouted, she who had never raised her quiet voice. After that nothing frightened her.

She searched hill and plain, mountain and valley. She took ship and sailed the seas, even beat on the doors of the Underworld to ask if her lover were there. From Pole to Pole and through the core of the Earth she searched.

And the gods watched from their mountaintop.

Psyche visited every temple, laying sacrifices on the altar, praying aloud for help to find her lover. At last she came to the temple of the goddess of love, and never suspecting Venus's hatred for her, went inside.

"No! Not there!" cried the gods out of Heaven, but Psyche did not hear.

"Oh dear goddess, loveliest of the Immortals, protector of all those who truly love. Help me find him! Help me, please!"

Behind her, Venus became gradually visible, like a spider's web in the morning dew. "There, there. I will, child, I will! Dry your tears! Of course I shall help you find your lover . . . Just one thing. *You must be my slave for seven years."*

Such torments and trials, such cruelties and dangers Venus poured on Psyche's lovely head that the gods on Olympus covered their eyes. For seven years Venus sent her slave on errands to the hearts of volcanoes, to the bottom of the sea. She sent her to winnow sand and to dig quicklime, to gather bird's eggs from cliffs and to sweep marshes dry. Psyche did it all.

And every day the gods liked Venus a little less and admired Psyche a little more.

"You see how she does everything that's asked of her!" said Cupid to Jupiter, King of gods.

"Someone's helping her, that's how," protested Venus sulkily. "She could never do it alone."

"You see how she brings a smile to the very faces of the Dead," said Cupid to Jupiter.

"Silence, son!" raged Venus. "It's you I sent to kill her in the first place! Why aren't you down there now, setting dogs on her trail, loosing monsters on to her scent?"

"Because I love her, Mother," said Cupid. All Heaven gasped in astonishment. *"Because it was I who rescued her. And it is I who have helped her survive your spite!"* He showed the three small burns on his chest, where

Psyche's oil lamp had spilled. "That's why I beg you, my Lord Jupiter: *make my love immortal!*"

All eyes turned to Jupiter, King of the gods.

"NO!" said Venus.

"YES!" boomed the god. "Thanks to Venus's cruelty, Psyche has earned her place among the Immortals. Marry her, Cupid, and when her mortal part falls away I shall set her in the night sky - a bouquet of stars in the arms of the night!"

That is how Psyche's long search ended. Cupid simply walked down from the foothills of Olympus and took her in his arms.

But what Cupid had forgotten - and Venus, too - was the monster Typhon. Woken and rising still from the seabed, with oily feathered wings of black it broke surface now, its thousand jaws snapping; it found no tasty morsel of mortal chained to the sea rock. So it dragged itself ashore, lumbered out of the sea, and came looking for its old enemies - the gods. Its search was a long one, longer than Psyche's. But at last it found a fitting prey: Venus, goddess of love, and her son Cupid.

They fled him far and fast, but when nothing else could save them, they changed themselves into little fishes and leapt up into the sky. Starry fishes, they swim still through the reefs of nebullae, the dark pools of space. And no fish in the ocean is as happy as Cupid, because Psyche is there too, as gentle and silent as a sea anemone caressing the liquid night.

The Armchair Traveller

AN INDIAN LEGEND

HE WAS NO beauty, it's true. In fact compared with his brother Karttikeya, his looks were downright bizarre. There was his colour, to begin with: blue is not to everyone's taste. Nor are four arms and a pot-belly. Nor are trunks and tusks. But then Ganesa's head *was* second-hand, his own having been cut off by Shiva in a moment of temper and replaced with the nearest one to hand, in the hope no one would notice. Even so, elephants are wise animals, and what Ganesa lacked in obvious good looks he made up for in wisdom. His library was huge. He read even more greedily than he ate, and he ate all day long.

Ganesa and his brother wanted to marry. Their sights were set on Siddhi and Buddhi. Although the obvious solution might seem that they should marry one each, fiery and quarrelsome Karttikeya saw things differently.

"I'll race you round the world, Ganesa," he said. "Whoever gets back first shall have them both!"

Ganesa munched on a pile of mangoes before answering. "That seems acceptable," he said, spitting pips out of the window. Never once did he lift his eyes from the book he was reading.

With no more luggage than his bow and arrows, Karttikeya leapt astride his trusty peacock (laughing aloud at the absurd idea of his fat, squat brother struggling round the globe behind him) and sped into the distance, a streamer of iridescent green and purple feathers and a flash of silver. He would be married and his first child born before Ganesa even got home!

"Well?" squeaked the mouse which lived somewhere between Ganesa's ears. It raced up and down his bony head. It shouted into his flappy ear. "Hurry! He's faster than you! Get moving!"

"All in good time," said Ganesa, and went on reading.

"Don't you *want* to marry Siddhi and Buddhi? They're lovely!"

"Intelligent, too," said Ganesa. "At least Buddhi is. Siddhi, I would estimate, is more of an achiever." He chewed slowly on a heap of melons while sucking strawberries up his trunk for later. "This really is an excellent book."

"No time for reading!" urged the mouse. "Aren't you even going to try? Don't you think you can do it? Karttikeya may be fast but you and I can push through jungles better than he. We could make up time in South America and Indonesia! Get on your feet! You won't win just sitting here!"

"Well, that's as maybe," said Ganesa through a mouthful of onions. "Let us not pre-judge these matters." His trunk reached out and took down another gigantic tome from his bookshelves. Then he settled back in his chair and shot peanuts into his open mouth with uncanny accuracy.

Round the fat world raced Karttikeya. He swam rivers, hacked his way through forests, and traipsed over fly-blown deserts. He saw the most wonderful cities in the world, some armour-plated with ice, some half-submerged in flowers and ivy. He met kings and climbed mountains. He watched harvests of wheat and seaweed and olives; he fought wild beasts with fur, with feathers, with scales. There was no time for wondering why the towers of Sumeria lay in ruins, or why the night sky sometimes

filled with trickling colours at the top of the world. He was too intent on winning, on beating his elephantine brother, on the stories that would be written of this epic race.

"Summon the musicians! Prepare the wedding feast! I am back! Karttikeya has returned!" His peacock looked bedraggled and tattered. Karttikeya was covered in dust, leaves and barnacles, and his clothes were full of sand. "Buddhi? Siddhi? . . . *You!*"

There sat Ganesa in his armchair, munching thoughtfully on cumquats and reading a copy of the *Puranas*. "Where have you been?" he asked his dishevelled brother. "We couldn't start the wedding without the bride-groom's brother."

Now Karttikeya, though he did not have the head of an elephant, was not altogether stupid. He suspected that Ganesa had not been *right round* the world, as he had. Indeed, he did not stop short of thinking Ganesa had never even levered his big rump out of that armchair. So he decided to shame him in front of Buddhi and Siddhi, and to show him up for a cheat.

"Tell us, brother. What did you think of China?"

"Which part?" replied Ganesa. "There's so much. The green pinnacles of the Yangtse, or the man-made marvels of Pekin?"

"Huh! . . . Was Siberia cold enough for you?" Karttikeya persisted.

"I preferred Greenland, myself - all that volcanic activity, those hot geysers - such astonishing shapes they make as the droplets freeze. And the fjords of Scandinavia - ah! - more indentations than the blade of a saw!"

"Since you were ahead of me," said Karttikeya sarcastically, "I'm surprised I didn't see the path you beat through the rainforests."

"Mmm, well, the forests regenerate so quickly," explained Ganesa. "That's why they've all but reclaimed those ziggurats. I notice a similarity - don't you? - between the ziggurats and the pyramids of Egypt. Do you suppose there is any truth in that story about Naramo-Sin sailing west with his mathematics?"

On and on Ganesa talked, pausing only to accept a grape from Buddhi, a pomegranate from Siddhi. The women sat at his feet spellbound by the pictures he painted of distant lands, their people, their philosophies, their legends. "I particularly like the Native American myth - so poetical in form. For instance . . ."

"All right! All right! You win!" said Karttikeya, slumping down, exhausted. "You win. You may have your brides."

Siddhi and Buddhi laughed and hugged each other with delight.

"Thank you, brother! How very gratifying!"

"But admit it, brother, just to me, just for the sake of history, *did* you really travel round the world?"

Ganesa tapped his bony skull with one of his four hands. "In my mind, dear brother. In my mind. You don't always have to visit a place to find out about it. That's why I treasure my books."

Buddhi and Siddhi gazed round them at the high shelves full of books and scrolls, and smiled as though they had just been given the world for a wedding present. Then they fetched Ganesa another hand of bananas and sat down to hear more stories.

Doctor Faust

A GERMAN LEGEND

FAUST, SAID his friends, was too clever for his own good. Faust, said his enemies, had no respect for God or religion. The truth was, Faust had a thirst for knowledge and would let nothing, friend nor enemy, stand in the way of his learning. So he took for granted nothing his parents told him, nor his teachers, nor even the priests. Instead, he read every book, consulted ancient charts and arts, and dabbled in chemistry.

Soon he could read the language of the stars and twelve other languages besides. Soon he could utter spells, work magic and, when he summoned up the Devil from Hell itself, the Devil came.

He came in the shape of a black dog with blazing red eyes and gaping jaws.

"Too ugly! Leave me!" Faust cried in commanding tones. "Come back in some other form, or I shall die of looking at you!" And the dog obediently turned and went. In that instant, Faust felt as powerful as God himself, for he could command the Devil and the Devil obeyed.

When the Devil reappeared, he called himself Mephistopheles and had a human shape, though his face was the saddest Faust had ever seen and there was a look in his eyes like a lost child. "Why do you summon me, Faust? What do you want?"

"Knowledge," said Faust. "Knowledge and power! Everything you can give me that plain, ignorant men cannot have!"

"I can give you that," said Mephistopheles. "But everything has a price. You won't want to pay mine."

"Name it!" said Faust, drunk with his own daring.

"Very well. For twenty-four years I serve you - do anything you ask, fulfil your every wish. After that time, I shall have your soul. Is that agreed?"

All his life Faust had been cleverer than anyone he met, able to outwit the sharpest wit. Here was a dog in human shape. Surely he could outwit him too - take the magic but keep his soul - especially after twenty-four years of learning to be cleverer still. "Agreed," he said.

From beneath his cloak, the Devil produced a scroll of paper. "Sign to it."

"Of course."

"In blood."

While the blood was still wet, Faust was already asking questions. How many stars? How large the universe? How old the sun? How does a bee fly? Who rules the universe?

"That last I shan't answer," said the Devil sulkily.

"Then God is greater than you?"

"Do you like pretty women?" asked Mephistopheles, changing the subject.

He fetched for Faust the most beautiful woman in the history of the world. (At least he fetched a likeness of her, which Faust could admire but not touch, an illusion rather than flesh and blood.) He played tricks on Faust's enemies. He did conjuring tricks for Faust's friends. Anything Faust could think to ask for, Mephistopheles did for him. Having seen the most beautiful woman in the world, of course, no other real, live woman could interest Faust. So he took no wife, no one who would care what became of him. But what did that matter? He had everything else.

He had more money than he could spend; houses and clothes, coaches and castles. But as for knowledge, all he found out was that facts bored him and the truth scared him: that good men went to Heaven, whereas bad men went to . . .

"Help me, books! How am I to trick my way out of this deal?" But his books told him nothing. "Help me, Wagner! How can I save my skin?" But his serving man did not know, and seeing Faust afraid of some impending doom, Wagner fled his master.

The days went by like bees on the wing, each stinging Faust into an awareness of his terrible predicament. Suddenly he was a middle-aged man, fat and slow from eating the Devil's rich food, lonely and bowed down under all the facts he knew. Faust's contract with Mephistopheles was due to expire, and suddenly Mephistopheles was not so harmless or helpful. Beyond his lonely, red-rimmed eyes, Faust could glimpse a

bottomless fiery pit bigger than the universe itself, a black-cogged machine whirring like the workings of an everlasting clock. At midnight, Faust must forfeit his soul to the Devil.

That last night, he considered the money, the laughter, the luxuries, the learning . . . and all of it seemed worthless alongside his little soul. He thought of hiding, of arguing, of pleading, but he knew that the Devil was coming to collect what was owed, and would not leave without it.

He barricaded the door, he loaded a gun, he stopped the clock. But time still moved on unstoppable. Ten o'clock, eleven, twelve. As the clock began to strike, Faust fell on his knees, sobbing and mouthing prayers. But the words turned to pitch in his mouth, and the contract in his pocket burned like phosphorus.

"Turn me into water drops and sprinkle me over the ocean," he prayed, "but don't let me fall into the Devil's hands! Don't let him take me to Hell!"

The clock in answer struck the twelfth stroke of midnight. Beneath the floorboards there was a roaring fire. Beyond the curls of smoke issuing between the floorboards, Mephistopheles stood - locked door or no locked door - holding the contract unfurled. The blood of Faust's signature was still wet . . .

"No. No! *No! No! NO!*"

Next morning Faust was nowhere to be found. Neighbours told of shrieks and cries, of lightning flashes and blood-red rain. But of Faust there was no trace, no bone, no hair. No books written, no sons or daughters to outlive him, no loyal friend to remember him. Nothing remained of the man who had been Faust; only wild stories of screaming in the night, and a slight smell of brimstone near the broken clock.

Alone

A NATIVE AMERICAN MYTH

A WOMAN lived on the shores of the sea. Her name was Copper Woman, though she was made of flesh and bones: flesh and bones and loneliness. One day she was so lonely that she wept, and then, to her shame, was seen weeping by a band of travelling women.

"Don't be ashamed, Copper Woman. Loneliness is not a crime; nor is crying," said the women. "There is even magic in a woman's tears. Didn't your crying fetch us here to cheer you?"

It was true. While the visitors stayed, Copper Woman was blissfully happy - talking, laughing, asking questions about the rest of the world, answering questions about her daily life.

"I catch bass here, gather seaweed there, and this is where the best shellfish grow. I made this dress from the silver skin of a seal, this soup from seaweed . . ."

But when the travelling women left, Copper Woman felt more lonely than ever, because now she knew how it felt not to be alone. She stood on the shore and wept, and her tears wetted the sand more than the sea ever had.

Remembering the magic the women had taught her, Copper Woman scooped the wet sand into a little shell and left it on the tide-line. By next day it had grown, not into any recognizable shape, but too large for the shell. So she transferred it to a sea-urchin's shell, then to a crab's. One day it reached out a tiny hand and clasped her finger tight, and would not let go, so that she had to carry it with her everywhere. She brought it shell-fish to eat and fish stock, gull-bones to play with as well as bright pebbles and seal's fur.

Copper Woman had given life to Sand Man, and when he was fully grown, his muscles were ropes of sand, strong to help with the fishing, tender to embrace her. Laughing with delight, she worked alongside her mate, chattering and singing, telling him all about herself and the shore-line, asking questions but never waiting for an answer, so glad was she of his company. They slept together in a big bed of sealskins, pillowed on gull feathers. His face was whiskery against hers, like a sea-lion's, and his chest had a soft, silvery fur. Copper Woman thought she would be happy for ever, now that she had a friend.

"I love you," she said, kissing her handsome Sand Man.

He smiled and turned towards her, his eyes bright with affection. He opened his mouth and she listened eagerly for him to say he loved her too.

But the only sound which emerged was the shrill cry of a seagull. *"Awwwkkhh! Awwwkkhh!"* Sand Man was, after all, the stuff of shells and birdbones and weed; of sand and tears and wishing. Copper Woman cried as she had never cried before, and was lonelier than she had been when she worked alongside the sobbing sea.

Bobbi Bobbi!

AN AUSTRALIAN MYTH

IN THE DREAMTIME, when the world was still in the making, the Ancient Sleepers rose from their beds and walked across sea and land, shaping the rocks, the plants, the creatures, arranging the stars to please the eye.

I remember. Or if not I, an ancestor of mine, or if not he, a sister of his ancestor. Our memories are blurred now, but we do remember: how the Ancient Sleeping spirits walked the Earth during Dream-time, and made things ready for us.

The snake spirit, Bobbi Bobbi, on his walk, heard crying and came upon a group of human beings newly brought to life.

"Does the world not please you for a place to live?" he asked.

"It would please us," sobbed the people, "if we were not so *hungry!*"

So Bobbi Bobbi searched his dreams for a kind of food, then gave it shape from a handful of soil. He made one flying bat and then another. Big they were, and meaty, each one a meal to feed a family. By the time Bobbi Bobbi walked on his way, over the brand-new world, the sky behind him was black with bats.

Binbinga lit a fire. Banbangi his sister crept up on a bat where it hung by its toes from a tree.

Crackle-rattle! The bat heard her, for its hearing was sharp and, just as she reached into the tree, it spread its leathery wings and flapped away.

Banbangi tended the fire. Binbinga took a stone and went to where the bats hung in a row by their toes from a cliff. He leaned back to throw.

Crackle-rattle! The bats heard him, for their hearing was keen, and just as he threw his stone, the bats spread their leathery wings and and flapped away.

Bobbi Bobbi, walking home through the red light of evening, heard crying. Once again, he came across the little new-made people - now looking more gaunt and desperate than before - and asked them what was wrong. But all they could do was point up at the sky at the flittering swarms of bats.

"We can't reach them. We can't catch them. All day we hunt them, but they won't be caught!"

Now Bobbi Bobbi was angry, because when he made a thing, he made it for a good purpose and not to find it fooling about in the red light of sunset. In his anger he beat his chest, till the ringing of his ribs gave him an idea.

With the sharp blade of the sickle moon, he cut a slit in the side of his chest, reached in his hand, and pulled out a rib, a single rib. Taking a squinnying aim on the circling bats, he flung the rib - it flew with a singing whistle - and tumbled a fine fat bat out of the blood-red sky!

The little people jumped and cheered, but not so high nor as loud as they jumped and cheered at what happened next. Bobbi Bobbi's rib-stick came whirling back out of the scarlet sky - right to his hand, right to the very palm of his hand!

Bobbi Bobbi gave his marvellous rib to the hungry newcomers and - wonder of wonders! - even when they threw it, it knocked the bats from the sky then swooped home again to their hands. "Boomerang", they called

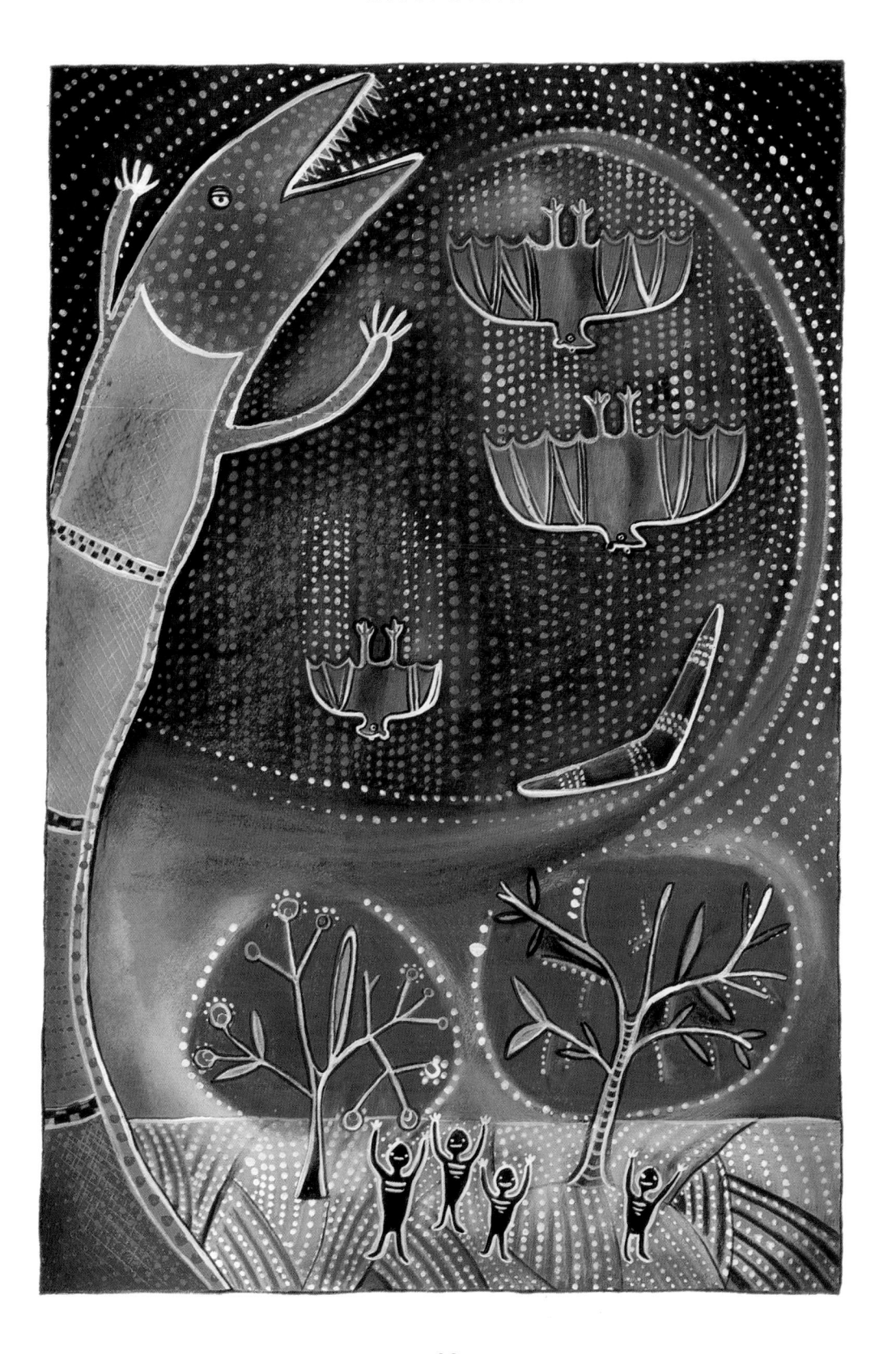

it, a treasure entrusted to them by the gods. A very piece of the gods.

No wonder they grew proud.

They knocked down more bats than they could eat, just to prove they could do it. The best throwers even boasted that they could knock down the birds . . .

". . . the clouds . . . !"

". . . the moon . . . !"

And as they strove to outdo one another, Binbinga threw the boomerang so hard and so high that he knocked a hole in the sky!

Down fell rubble and blue dust, on to the ground below. Winds escaped through the gap, stars showed at midday, and the handiwork of the Ancient Sleepers was spoiled.

Now Bobbi Bobbi was really angry, because when he made a thing, he made it to good purpose, not to see it played with by fools.

Before the boomerang could arc back through the tear in the sky, Bobbi Bobbi reared up, caught it in his mouth and shook it with rage.

"Quick! Before he swallows it!" cried Binbinga.

"He mustn't take it from us!" cried Banbangi. And they ran at the great snake spirit, scrambled up his scaly body, clambered up his trunk towards the broad, toothless rim of his mouth. They each took hold of one end of the precious boomerang. In their ignorance, they actually tried to pull it out of Bobbi Bobbi's mouth!

But the snake spirit only dislocated his jaw (as snakes can) to widen the gape of his cavernous jaw, and swallowed Binbinga and Banbangi, swallowed them whole.

A great silence fell over the newly made world, broken only by the *rattle-crack* of the last remaining bats.

For a long while, the flying bats cruised the sky above the new-made people. Daily they increased in number, just as the hunger increased in the bellies of those below. When, at last, Bobbi Bobbi relented and gave back the rib-stick, it was only in exchange for their promises to use it as it was meant to be used – for catching food.

The Gingerbread Baby

A MYTH FROM PALESTINE

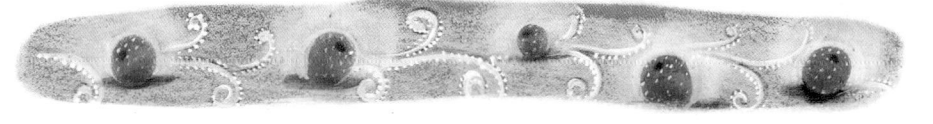

LEILA PUT in the bread and closed the oven door. She drew a deep breath and sighed; there was sea-salt in the air. "While the bread bakes, I just have time to stroll down to the harbour," she thought. "I must see the sea today."

Down at the waterfront, a ship was loading. Leila had no sooner stepped aboard than it set sail, and carried her over three oceans and five high seas till she came to a land rather like her own. Down by the docks, the houses were shabby and the people poor. A home was one room and a meal was one raisin and the reason was poverty.

A young widow stood by her door, big-bellied with yet another baby, and weeping fit to break your heart. "Another mouth to feed," she said, "and where's the food to come from? Even our poor dog is starving to death."

Leila wished she had brought the loaf of bread with her, for truly this whole family was as thin as a bunch of twigs. The dog, too. As it was, Leila felt in the pockets of her gown and there was not so much as a coin for her to give the widow.

Higher up, the houses were large and beautiful, each room as big as a lesser man's house, each meal a marvel, and the reason was wealth. Even so, a woman stood on her golden balcony and wept fit to break your heart.

"What's the matter?" asked Leila.

"Nothing your kindness can cure, old lady," sobbed the woman. "My husband the sultan hates me, because I have given him no children!"

"*He* has given *you* no children, you mean!" said Leila. "These men! How they complain about the least thing! You dry your tears and let an old lady advise you." She whispered in the sultana's ear, and the young woman, though she shook her head - "It will never work!" - did just as she was told.

When the sultan came home, she told him, to his great joy, that she was expecting a baby. Then, every day, Leila padded the sultana's dress a little more, so that she really did look as though she had told him the truth. Meanwhile, each day, Leila also cooked a morsel of gingerbread, and took it down to the garden gate and fed it to a bony little dog who poked his nose through the bars.

After eight months, Leila went to the kitchen and made more dough than usual. She pinched the gingerbread into the size and shape of a baby, and baked it in the palace oven, wondering as she did so, if her own bread at home was baked yet.

Every day, the sultan came asking, "Is the child born yet?" At last he heard the words he longed for. Leila peeped round the bedroom door and told him, "Your dear wife has given you a beautiful child, your eminence. As soon as she is strong enough, she will bring the boy to you in the garden."

There, amid the tinkling fountains and orange trees, the sultan sat singing for sheer joy. Watching from her balcony, the sultana cradled her gingerbread baby . . . and sobbed fit to break your heart. "Did you really think he would be fooled, Leila?" she wept. "Do you think my husband is blind and stupid? It is a lovely baby you baked for me, but anyone with two eyes and a nose can tell it's made of gingerbread!"

"Yes, indeed," said Leila happily. "Anyone with two eyes a nose and a tail." She told the sultana to go down to her husband, carrying the child. "But not too tight, you hear?"

Leila ran downstairs ahead of her, ran to the garden gate where every day she had fed the bony dog. Sure enough, the dog was there again today and, at the smell of gingerbread wafting over the gardens, began to drool. Leila unlatched the gate . . .

"I come, O husband, to show you our lovely child," said the sultana, her voice full of fright.

The sultan sniffed. "Well, he *smells* better than most babies," he said.

Just then, with a flash of fur, one bark and a rattle of skinny bones, a dog bounded over the fountain and seized the "baby" in its mouth.

"Call the guard! Shut the gates! Stop that dog!" yelled the sultan desperately. But no one was quick enough to catch the mongrel with its

meal of gingerbread wrapped in priceless lace. The dog ran straight home - down to the docks - and shared its good fortune with the widow and her hungry, fatherless children.

The crumbs were still falling when Leila hurried in, breathless from the long trot. She went straight to the box in the corner (which was all the widow had for a cradle) and lifted out the tiny, half-starved baby boy crying there with hunger. "Listen," said Leila. "How would you like your baby to live in a palace, with all the food he can eat, growing up loved and safe, to be a sultan one day?"

"Better than words can say," said the widow. "But how?"

"Trust me," said Leila. Picking up the beautiful white shawl from the floor, she wrapped the real baby in it and carried him out to where the palace guards were searching the streets.

"All is well!" she said. "This family rescued the baby before the dog could hurt him."

When the sultan heard that, he gave command that the widow should receive a reward - a reward so huge that the family need never go hungry again. And hugging the baby boy to his chest, he carried it home to his wife.

Imagine the sultana's surprise, having lost a gingerbread baby, when she got back a real live son. She was too happy to quibble.

Leila sniffed the air and smelled baking bread. "Time I was going," she said, and climbed aboard a ship making ready to sail. Over three oceans and five high seas it carried her, to the harbour below her own little house. As she opened the door, the wonderful smell of baking bread greeted her like a friend. "Just in time," she said, and taking her loaf out of the oven, cut herself a slice to eat with a glass of hot, sweet tea.

The Price of Fire

A MYTH FROM GABON, WEST AFRICA

FROM THE LEAFY canopy of the forest hang the long, looping lianas, leafy ropes of creeper like tangled hair. Within the loop of the longest liana, God used to sleep away the hottest part of the day, swinging in his viny hammock. His mother said the climb was too tiring now, so she dozed on a tree stump down below, remembering.

The dark damp of the forest floor is a chilly place, especially for an old lady. So God invented fire to keep Grandma God warm: a morsel of sun, a kindling of twigs, and there it was one day, crackling merrily and casting an orange glow.

Manwun came shivering down the forest paths, looking for berries. He saw the fire, saw God's mother asleep in its glow, and thought, "I could use that stuff to keep *me* warm." So he stole the fire, and ran for home as fast as he could manage with an armful of burning twigs.

Grandma God stirred, shivering, and bleated up into the trees, "Son! Son! Someone has stolen my fire!"

God leapt from his hammock at once and, using the ropes of creeper, swung from tree to tree with a piercing yell. He quickly caught up with the thief, swooping low over his head and snatching back the stolen fire.

But Manwun went home and told his village about fire. Soon Mantoo came creeping by and, waiting till Grandma God fell asleep, stole the fire from in front of her. She dreamed of ice, and the chattering of her teeth woke her. "Son! Son! Someone has stolen my fire!"

Swingng hand-over-hand, from tree to tree, God went after the thief, and though Mantoo had almost reached the edge of the forest, he too felt the red-and-yellow treasure snatched from his grasp as God went swooping by with a whoop of triumph.

"We could just *ask* him for some fire," suggested Woman, but no one listened to her.

Manthree made careful plans before he left for the forest. He knew that God would be on the look-out for sneak-thieves creeping through the undergrowth. So he sewed together a coat of feathers – one from every kind of bird – and practised hour after hour. First he jumped from logs, then from branches, then from hilltops, until he could fly with all the skill and speed of a bird.

Dozing on his liana swing, all God saw was a flash of colour as Manthree went by. He never suspected a bird-man had swooped on Grandma God's fire and snatched it up, kindling and all.

"Son! Son! Someone has stolen my lovely fire!" she bleated, and God gave a weary sigh, for he had done enough chasing for one day.

Swinging hand-over-hand, whooping from tree to tree, God went after Manthree: he could just make out the glimmer of orange and red among the treetop fruits. Quick as a swallow, Manthree darted between the dense trees. He reached the edge of the forest and burst out into the bright sunlight of the plain, soaring and looping over rivers and valleys. Out in

the open, God had to make chase on foot, wading and jumping, running and climbing, till at last, he sprawled exhausted on a sunny hillside to catch his breath. "All right! All right! You may have fire! The day is too hot and the world too big for me to chase you any more. Have it and be done!"

Manthree (whose feathers were starting to char from carrying the fire) gave a great cheer, and took his prize home. God, on the other hand, dragged his feet all the weary way back to the forest.

"I've given them the fire, Mother!" he called as he approached the tangle of lianas and the dark, damp tree stumps beneath. "I decided they could have some too. It will set the world twinkling at night, and their cooking will taste better. Was I right, do you think? I'll make you some more, of course. Mother? Mother?"

Grandma God lay curled up beside the circle of ash where her fire had once burned. She was cold as death, and no fire would ever warm her again.

First God wept, then he swore to make Manwun, Mantoo, Manthree and the rest pay for stealing fire from his poor, frail old mother. "When I made them, I meant them to live for ever. But now, for doing this, let them taste the cold of Death! Let every man, woman and child grow old and cold and die!"

So that is why old folk complain of the cold, and shiver on the warmest days, and why, at last, the flame of life gutters and goes out in their eyes, no matter how close they make their beds to the campfire.

Sea Chase

A FINNISH MYTH

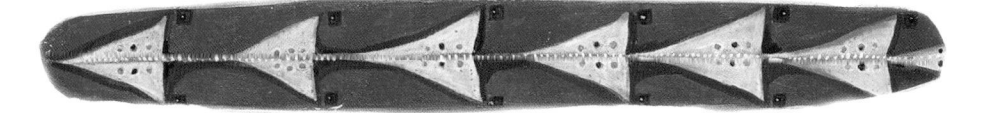

ILMARINEN the blacksmith knew that only one gift would be good enough to win him the daughter of Lady Louhi of Lapland for his bride. He did not know what it was, but he knew it would be his best work. So he took a swan's feather, a cup of milk, a bowl of barley and a strand of wool, and forged them in his furnace into a single magical gift.

The first time he opened the furnace door he found a golden bowl. But he broke that between his hands and threw the pieces back into the fire, fuelling the furnace even hotter. The next time he opened the door, he found a red copper ship, perfect in every detail. But he crushed that between his hands and threw it back into the flames, fuelling the furnace hotter still. The third time he found a little cow with golden horns; the fourth a plough with silver handles. But none of these things was good enough to win the consent of Lady Louhi. For she ruled the Northland, where the ice growls and night lasts all day and the halls are hung with icicles, like Lady Louhi's heart.

The fifth time Ilmarinen opened the furnace door he found - a something: a sampo. He did not know what it was, but he knew it was the best thing he had ever made. So he sailed with it to the Northland in a boat of copper, and won the daughter of Louhi for his wife. Lady Louhi took the sampo and built for it a hollow copper hill whose door locked with a dozen keys, and inside the hill the sampo worked, its lid whirled and its magic flowed into the icebound ground . . .

Sadly, Ilmarinen's bride was no sooner won than lost again. She died, melted away in his arms like ice in spring. So he went back to the Lady Louhi and asked for her second daughter.

"No!" said Louhi. "You have squandered one treasure of mine; shall I see you squander another?"

"Then give me back my sampo," said Ilmarinen. "I have not had its worth in wives."

"Give me back my daughter and I shall give you back your sampo," said Lady Louhi bitterly. "Not before."

Ilmarinen could see why she would not part with the sampo. Since his last visit, Lapland had changed past all recognition. Where there had been snowfields, now barley waved golden and ripe. Where once only reindeer and husky dogs had left their tracks in the snow, fat cows and sleek horses grazed in flowery meadows. And where icicles had hung from the eaves of Louhi's cabin, golden ornaments tinkled in a balmy breeze. Only now did Ilmarinen begin to understand just what a wonder he had made.

Boldly, Ilmarinen seized Louhi's second daughter, flung her over his shoulder and ran for the shore. But though he got clean away, he had sailed only five leagues when the girl, before his very eyes, turned into a seagull and flapped back to land.

By the time Ilmarinen reached his Finnish home, he had abandoned all idea of marrying. All he could think of was getting back the sampo. "I made it, after all," he complained to wise old Väinämöinen.

"Then we should share in its magic," the old man agreed.

Three heroes set sail that summer: and three more different men Finland never forged. There was good old Väinämöinen, sensible and sage; Ilmarinen, dogged and strong; and Lemminkäinen, rash and passionate as a fool in love. With three at the oars, the little boat fairly leapt through the waves.

... Too fast for the health of the Giant Pike who lay in wait. Bandit of the sealanes, it plundered the high waves for whale and sturgeon, seizing them in its jaws and eating them, bone and caviar. But when it gaped to swallow the boat of Väinämöinen, the ship's bow rammed it, the proud prow pierced it ... and the heroes ate pike for five days. Out of the jawbone, Väinämöinen made himself a kantele – a kind of harp with bones for strings; he used the teeth to pluck a tune. And so it was to the sound of music that they came to Pohjola. In place of a beach, huge copper rollers lay at the water's edge for rolling ships in and out of the freezing sea. Beyond the rollers, between the pine trees where day-long dark had once clung, the sun now dazzled on Louhi's cabin and on the copper hill. A gull swooped down and pecked Ilmarinen on the head.

"What brings you here?" asked Lady Louhi, bare armed in the balmy warmth of her cabin's porch.

"The joy of your company and the sampo which has made your frosty land a paradise," said Väinämöinen. "Since Finland made it, shan't Finland enjoy its magic too? Let us share!"

But the sun had done nothing to melt the ice in Lady Louhi's heart. "Can one squirrel live in two trees?" she said. "Lapland has the sampo now and no one shall take it from us!"

If Väinämöinen was annoyed, he did not show it. He simply took out the kantele - the pike-jaw harp - and began to play. The music was sweeter than mead, the notes softer than snowflakes on the lids of those listening. Louhi made to rise from her chair, but fell back, as all around her the lords and ladies, the soldiers and slaves of the Northland slumped down asleep.

The three heroes tiptoed past them, up to the copper hill. Ilmarinen pushed butter in the keyholes of the dozen locks, while Väinämöinen sang strange and low wordless songs. The door swung open, and the sampo was theirs!

One side was grinding out fair harvests, one peace, one wealth, while the bright lid spun amid a galaxy of sparks.

Past the cabin, over the copper rollers, out into the surf went the three brave raiders, dipping their oars as softly as wings, stealing away from the Northland. But Lemminkäinen was bursting with pride and pleasure. "We should celebrate!" he declared. "We should sing!"

"No. We should not," said Väinämöinen in a whisper. But Lemminkäinen would not be told.

"We came and we stormed the copper hill!
And now we'll sing till the sun stands still
How Finland's heroes stole the Mill
Of Happiness, and took their fill!"

A crane roosting on a sea rock rose lazily in the air and flapped inland. It flew to the cabin of Lady Louhi; it woke the Lapps from their magic sleep. "The Finns have opened the copper hill! The Finns have stolen the sampo! Arise and give chase!"

Over the copper rollers thundered the Lapp ship - huge as a castle, with a hundred men at the oars and a thousand standing. And Louhi at the stern cursed as she held the tiller:

"Come, you Mist-moisty Maiden!
Come from the seabed, Gaffa's child!
Stormclouds with thunder laden,
Come and turn the calm sea wild!"

A hundred miles away, Väinämöinen's boat was suddenly wrapped in mist as thick as sheep's wool. Lemminkäinen's song, first muffled then stifled, fell silent. The three heroes could not see as far as each other's faces; they might as well have been alone on the wide ocean. Without sight of the stars, how could they steer a course for home? Without sight of the sea, how could they avoid the reefs and shoals of shallow water?

Väinämöinen picked up the kantele and began to play. If the mist were magic, so was his music. For the fog began to glow and gleam, to run and steam. It turned to a golden liquor which poured into the sea, a cataract of honey. Lemminkäinen opened his mouth and swallowed the sweetness greedily. Ilmarinen wiped his sticky hands and pulled on his oar. The sea ahead was clear, the water round them a puddle of honey, astonishing the fish.

But Louhi and her men had gained ground.

A mile farther, and the sea around Väinämöinen's boat began to seethe. Out of a geyser of bubbles burst the murderous great head of a sea monster. With scales of slate and teeth of razorshell, the oldest child of Gaffa the Kraken broke surface and gaped its jaws to bite the boat in two.

Väinämöinen threw his cloak, and as the monster chewed it to rags, leaned out over the water and took hold. His fingers pinching both the green frilled ears, he hoisted Gaffa's child high out of the water and hooked it to the mast by its earlobes. The boat sat low in the water and filled up with a terrible smell, but as the monster dried in the sun, its roars subsided to whimpering.

"Tell us, O Gaffa's child, why you have come," said Väinämöinen (though while he spoke, Louhi was gaining ground).

"The Lady Louhi conjured me to kill you," sobbed the monster, "but if you let me down, you may go on your way for all I care."

What a splash the creature made as it hit the water; for some time it lay

rubbing its ragged ears. They were watching it still when the storm came up behind them, and the clouds began to hurl lightning and thunderbolts. The sea rose, the sea rolled, the sea writhed into waves like spires of spume. One after another the pitchy waves beat against the little boat, washing over the low rails, filling the bilges with saltwater and chips of ice. A few more waves, and the boat would founder. Lemminkäinen had no breath left to sing: he was too busy baling.

One wave, bigger than all the rest, crashed down on their heads and washed the pike-jaw harp out of Väinämöinen's hands, washing it over the side, sinking it in six thousand fathoms.

Väinämöinen's lips, wet and cold and trembling with sadness at the loss of his harp, would not pucker at first. But he wiped them dry and whistled long and low - a noise so loudly magic that it brought all the way from the cliffs of Finland the great Sea Eagle whose wings span Bear Island and whose beak made the fjords. From its tail Lemminkäinen pulled two feathers the size of castle walls and battened them to the boat's sides; so high that the sea could not break over them, so glossy that the boat slipped all the faster through the vertiginous seas.

But meanwhile, Louhi and her men had gained more ground.

The heroes looked back and thought they saw a cloud. They looked

back and thought they saw a flock of birds. They looked back and knew they were seeing a ship as huge as a castle, crammed with warriors. Suddenly Louhi was on them: a hundred men pulling on a hundred oars and a thousand more standing.

Väinämöinen fumbled in his pocket. He pulled out his tinderbox and from it took a sliver of flint. Over his left shoulder he threw it, as you or I throw spilled salt, and as he did so, he sang:

"Grow reef, and crack their prow;
Rocks arise to rack them - now!"

The tiny shard grew to a pebble, the pebble to a stone, the stone to a boulder, the boulder multiplied a millionfold. A reef grew in that instant, so sheer and sharp that it slashed the sea to foam.

Too late Louhi saw it lying across her path. The hull shook and the hundred rowers fell from their benches while the thousand warriors sprawled in the bilges. Seams parted, planks splintered and the sea surged in. As her ship fell apart round her, Louhi clapped the clinker sides under her arms, the rudder under her coat-tails, and telling her men, "Cling tight to me!", the Lady Louhi took flight.

She became an eagle of wood and bone, with talons forged from swords and a beak from axeheads. With a shriek of hatred, she swooped on Väinämöinen's boat out of the north-western sky, one wingtip sweeping the sea, the other brushing the clouds.

"Oh for a cloak of fire now, to keep off this fearful bird!" muttered the old hero, and he called out, "One last time I say, let us share the sampo! Let's share its magic!"

"No! I won't share it! I shan't share it!" shrieked the woman-eagle plumed with soldiers, and her metal talons snatched the sampo out of Ilmarinen's lap.

So Väinämöinen pulled his oar out of its rowlock and, whirling it three times round his head, struck out at the swooping eagle of wood and bone. Plank and men and weapons showered down. The wood wings buckled, the tail feathers dropped their burden of men into the sea. But the sampo

- oh the sampo! - it fell from her claws into the green, seething sea!

The three heroes leapt to their feet in horror. The Lady Louhi soared into the cloudbanks with a terrible cry. Only the lid of the marvellous sampo dangled from her finger. "I'll knock down the moon!" she ranted. "I'll wedge the sun in a cleft of cliff! I'll freeze the marrow in your bones for this, thieving Finns!"

Väinämöinen tossed his long grey hair defiantly. "You may do much, Louhi! God knows, you have done enough! But the sun and moon are God's, and beyond your reach and mine. Here our battle ends, and here our ways part!"

The enemies turned in opposite directions: Väinämöinen to the south, Louhi to the north. The Lapland she found on her return was very different from the one she had left. Silent, sunless and clogged with snow, groaning under the weight of hard-packed ice, it was once again home to wolves and bears. Only the magic of the sampo's lid brought back the herds of reindeer out of the gloomy forests, brought singing to the lips of the drovers, and pride to the Lapp nation who live at the top of the world.

The three heroes rowed home. No singing now from Lemminkäinen, for the sampo was lost and so was the magical harp. "The best and the last I shall ever make," said Väinämöinen mournfully.

But whether by accident of tide, or whether by order of the sea king Ahto (in thanks for the new harp he cradled on his lap), something wonderful greeted them, bright amid the seaweed and shells of the beach. Pieces of the marvellous sampo had washed up on the Finnish shore, and with them better fortune than the Finns had ever known. From then on, the harvests grew taller in the fields, the beasts fatter, the treasury fuller, the people happier than they had ever been before. Poets, most of all, found the air aswarm with words, and dreamed their greatest verses - sagas of sampos, heroes and the sea.

Young Buddha

AN INDIAN LEGEND

SWEET AND PURE as dewfall on a spring morning, Queen Maya was loved by her husband and people as much as any goddess. One night, she dreamed that an elephant, white as milk, raised its trunk in salute over her. In her dream, its phantom whiteness came closer and closer, trumpeting, moving right through her own transparent body. When she woke, she was expecting a child. With such a beginning, no ordinary boy. His very name meant "bringer of good".

From the first moment, Prince Gautama was remarkable. He was no sooner born than he took seven steps, looked around him at the astonished waiting-women and midwives, and said, "This is the last time I shall come."

He understood, you see, without anyone teaching him, how life goes round and round, each soul quitting one body only to be born afresh in another: each life a new chance to strive for perfection, to escape the endless treadmill of rebirth. But despite his childish wisdom Gautama was as ignorant as any other newborn baby of the world outside his nursery.

"One day he will give up his kingdom!" cried a woman of such age and wisdom that her milky old eyes could see into the future. "He will be a mighty teacher, greatest of all the teachers, bringing peace to countless millions!"

"Oh no, he won't!" cried the King, for Gautama was his son and his intended heir. He wanted for Gautama what every father wants - a life of ease, a life of pleasure, a life of plenty. "My son shall be happy!" said the King.

So, when Prince Gautama went out for a chariot ride, crowds of people lined the streets: healthy, well-fed, handsome people with smiling faces. Anyone ugly, anyone crippled or pocked by disease, anyone starving or threadbare or weeping was swept off the street, along with the dung and the litter, by squads of royal guardsmen.

The King found his son a beautiful girl to be his wife, and filled the palace with music, fountains and works of art. For all the young Prince knew, the whole world was a paradise of joy and unfailing loveliness. The gods above shook their heads and frowned.

One day, despite the efforts of the royal guards, despite the King's commands . . . and because the gods care only for the truth, Gautama went riding in his chariot. And he saw an old man, wrinkled and bent and weary from a lifetime of work.

"Who is he? *What* is he?" Gautama asked his chariot driver. "I have never seen the like."

Then the chariot driver could not help but explain: how everything - people and animals and plants - grow old and feeble and lose their first, youthful bloom. It is the truth; what else could the poor man say? When Gautama got home that day, he did a great deal of thinking.

Next day, despite the efforts of the soldiers, despite the King's commands, and because the gods care only for the truth, Gautama went riding again. And he saw a woman with leprosy lying beside the road, hideous and racked with pain.

"Who is she? *What* is she?" Gautama asked his chariot driver. "I have never seen the like."

Then the chariot driver could not help but explain: how sometimes people and animals and plants get sick and suffer pain or are born disabled or meet with terrible injuries which scar and mar their bodies. It is the truth; what else could the poor man say? Before he fell asleep that night, Gautama did a great deal of thinking.

Next day, despite the royal guards, despite the King, and because the gods care only for the truth, Gautama saw a dead body lying unburied at the roadside. "What is that?" Gautama asked his chariot driver, seized with clammy horror. Then the chariot driver could not help but explain: how everything, everyone dies. It is the truth; what else could he say? Before the moon set that night, Gautama was a changed man.

He no longer took any pleasure in the dancing girls who tapped their tambourines and shook the golden bells at their ankles. He had no appetite for the delicious meals, no patience with the games he had once played. Taking a horse from the stable, he rode like a madman, searching for some solace in the great empty countryside beyond the city wall.

But as he rode, it seemed to him that the very fields were screaming under the sharp ploughshares of the farmers; that the woodsmen were breaking the spines of the trees with their merciless axes; that the insects in the air and worms in the soil were crying, crying, dying . . .

In a lonely glade, under the shade of a rose-apple tree, Gautama found a measure of peace. Like a man balancing a million plates, he reached a perfect stillness and balance. He saw the whole, how the world was, with all its evil, and he perceived that somewhere beyond its noisy hurtling waterfall of misery - if he could just reach through the crashing torrent - there was a place of peace and stillness.

Giving away all his jewels, all his possessions, he left his father, left his wife, left even his young son. It was no easier for him to leave them than it was for them to lose him but as he told them, "It is the fear and pain of such partings that make life unbearable. That's why I have to go and discover a different kind of life untouched by any such sorrow."

• • •

In his search for understanding, Gautama tried to go without food and drink, to ignore his body so that his mind could fly beyond and away from it. But starving himself only left him sleepy and weak and his thoughts cloudy and muddled. And so he bathed his poor, bony body in the river and the riverside trees reached down their branches in sheer love, to help him from the water. Gautama took food.

Later, as he walked through the forest, a giant snake, king of its breed, reared up before him, its head as high as the tallest tree. "Today! Today, O wisest of men, you shall have what you desire! Today you will become a Buddha!"

So sitting himself down, cross-legged, under a holy tree, Gautama vowed that he would not move once more until he had grasped the reason for life itself. He practised meditation, freeing his mind like a bird from a cage, to soar through past, present and future, through place and time and all the elements.

At the sound of his whispered chanting, Mara, god of passion, fretted and raged and fumed and quaked. He summoned his sons and daughters, his troops and his weapons. *"Destroy him!"* he commanded. "If he finds a way to rid the world of Wanting and Longing and Anger and Ambition and Greed and Fright I shall have no empire left, no more power than a blade of dead grass trodden underfoot!" At Mara's command, Thirst and Hunger, Anger and Joy and Pride and Discontent all hurled themselves at the fragile, silent, solitary man seated under the tree.

But they might as well have hurled themselves against rocks, for Gautama was beyond their reach, out of their range, his soul united with the gods, his thoughts as large as the Universe. Gautama had become a Buddha. And now, when the very word "Buddha" is spoken, *his* is the face which fills a million minds, with its knowing, tender, smiling peace.

The Battle of the Drums

A NATIVE AMERICAN MYTH

THERE WERE magical marks on his forehead, and magic in the way he grew - from baby to child in the beat of a heart, from child to youth in another. Lone Man had magical powers, so when he wanted a thing he was inclined to take it. He wanted a coat, and Spotted Eagle Hoita had one, a fine white one. Lone Man whistled up the wind and sent it to blow on Hoita, and the white hide coat was whisked from his back and carried away, away and away.

It blew through the arch of a rainbow which touched it with seven colours along with a glisten of dew. When travellers found it, they said, "This is so beautiful it must belong to Lone Man."

So Lone Man came by his coat, but in doing so, he made an enemy. For Hoita *knew* the coat was his. And Hoita also knew how to bear a grudge.

Soon afterwards, there came from the north the beat of a drum like the thud of a heart. It woke the animals on the plain, and stirred them to their feet - every buffalo and dog, every quail and coney and mouse. Every day, Lone Man saw them pass by his home - a huge migration of animals, their colours fading to a whiteness, their white forms fading into the northerly distance. Then his stool stirred its three legs and walked away, whitewash white, along with his hogan and hives, his fishing rod and shoes.

Day and night: *thum-thum-thum*. Night and day: *thum-thum-thum*. Powerless to resist, the animals moved north towards the sound, towards the place called Dog Den. When even the growing things on the plain began to grow pale, Lone Man knew he must act before his people starved. So he turned himself into a little white hare, and loped away north in the footprints of the rest.

When he reached Dog Den, the noise of drumming filled the air from snow to sky, from drift to cloud, filled Lone Man's long ears and set his long

feet thumping. There was Hoita, leading the animals in a dance, chanting out famine, chanting out strife.

> "Lone Man shall have his coat;
> Lone Man shall have no more;
> Lone Man shall have no food or joy
> From hill to shining shore."

The drum Hoita beat was a huge roll of hide taken from the largest buffalo in the world.

> "Lone Man shall have no luck;
> Lone Man shall have no chance;
> Lone Man shall have no powers at all
> While Hoita leads the dance."

Now Lone Man knew what he must do: find a drum bigger and more magical than Hoita's. He searched the world over, then he searched the world under, and there he found the two Turtles who swim with the Earth on their back, balancing the world on their shells.

"If I were to beat on your shells," said Lone Man, "I could raise magic enough to overpower Spotted Eagle Hoita."

"If you were to beat on our shells, the world might tumble from our backs and sink into the Waters like a stone in a pond," replied the Turtles. "But you are quite right. Our shape has magic enough. Look carefully, Lone Man, and copy what you see."

So Lone Man felled an oak tree and built a frame. He took the hides of a hundred buffaloes, and stretched them over the oak frame. And he made a drum the shape of an Earth Turtle, and almost as big. When he beat it, the sea quaked, the sky vibrated, the hills jumped and hopped like fleas around the plain. It sounded like the heartbeat of the Earth itself.

"What is that sound?" said Hoita, far away at Dog Den in the north. "Go and see, Coyote."

So Coyote went to see what was making the noise. But Lone Man was waiting, and put a lead round his neck.

"What *is* that sound?" said Hoita. "Go and see, Birds." So the Birds went to see what was making the sound. But Lone Man was waiting with nuts and seed, to feed them.

"WHAT *IS* THAT SOUND?" demanded Hoita. "Go and see, Buffaloes." So the Buffaloes went to see what was making the noise, and the magic of the Great Drum scattered them across the Great Plain, scattered them once again within reach of Lone Man's hungry people, where they were needed most.

The Hoita realized that the sound was not the Earth's heartbeat but the beat at the heart of Lone Man's magic, and he let all the animals go, sent them south again, to recover their colours and roam the lands of Lone Man and his kin.

Spotted Eagle Hoita had glimpsed the future, and knew how much the plains people were going to need Lone Man.

"Lone Man shall need my coat;
Lone Man shall need his lance.
The dangers ahead are many
For this leader of the dance!"

The Golden Vanity

AN ENGLISH LEGEND

THE PENNONS at the masthead were new, the gold paint on the figurehead gleaming, and the sailors were still thinking of home when it happened. Not three weeks out of Portsmouth the *Golden Vanity* was overtaken by a Turkish caravel, light and fast and with guns enough to send the ship and all its crew to the bottom of the sea.

Slow and ponderous, the great English treasure galleon wallowed on the swell, while stone balls and chain-shot smashed away the spars and rigging like twigs falling from a tree. "We're lost! We're taken!" groaned the Captain, and he cursed his crew, his vessel and the admiral who had sent him on this fatal voyage.

Up jumped the cabin boy, Billy. "There's something I could do, sir! There's something I could try! What would you say to me sinking the

Turk deep down where the whale bones lie?"

"I'd say five thousand pounds and marry my daughter," said the Captain surlily, "but since when did cabin boys win battles?"

From his belt Billy pulled a little bradawl, a tool for boring holes in wood. "What say I swam across and holed the Turks under the waterline let in the sea to wet their heathen feet?"

The Captain threw aside his spyglass and turned to look at the boy for the first time. "Reckon you could do it?"

"He can if anyone can!" exclaimed the second mate. "The lad swims like a fish, he does!"

Cannonfire like the crack of lightning rived the smoky air, and a ball whistled by the Captain's ear. He put out a paw and clasped Billy's little hand in his. "Then do your best for us, son, and do your worst to them!"

They tied a rope round Billy's waist and lowered him into the sea: he trembled like a fish on a line. But no sooner was he in the water than he untied the rope and struck out strongly, gliding through the wavetops like a very porpoise. "Tell your daughter I shall buy her a fine house with five thousand pounds!" he called back with a laugh.

The water was cold. Now and then it exploded into spray as a cannon-ball fell short or a piece of rigging crashed down into the sea. But by closing his eyes and imagining – Billy the Beau! Little Billy Gentleman! – he somehow reached the Turkish hull. She had heaved-to to empty her cannon into the *Golden Vanity*, and the hull stood still in the choppy ocean. Holding his breath, he dived – clawed away the pitch and tallow coating, and bored through the wooden hull.

Again and again Billy dived, until his lungs were burning and his body blue with cold. Not until he heard the cries aboard the caravel – "Awash! Awash! We're holed!" – did he push the bradawl back into his belt and begin the long swim back.

Chilled to the marrow and tired past all enduring, Billy closed his eyes and thought of his mother's face the day he rode to church in a carriage, to marry the Captain's daughter; frock coat of red velvet, with a spyglass and a shiny sword, his brothers would say, "There goes our little Billy; he

69

saved the day, you know!" When he opened his eyes again, the hull of the *Golden Vanity* loomed huge above him, steep as a cathedral wall.

"Throw down a rope, Captain!" he called, and saltwater slopped into his throat. "I can't . . . much longer . . . so tired."

"Raise the topsail and let's put on some speed, men!" said the Captain on his bridge.

The crew stared at him. They ran to the rail. They pointed to Billy, in case the Captain had not heard him. Someone ran for a longer rope.

"Billy did no more than his duty, and now you can do yours," barked the Captain. "Man the yard-arms, or I'll blow your heads off for scurvy mutineers!" And he actually primed his hand pistols, then and there. As he did so, he muttered, "Does he think I have money and daughters to spare on the likes of him?"

"For the love of God, Captain! Keep your money and keep your daughter! But pull me up or I'm dead and done for!" called Billy.

The Captain pursed his thin lips, put his spyglass to his eye and watched the crow's-nest of the Turkish ship sink with a fountaining flurry beneath the cold sea waves. "Lay on more canvas, men," he said.

Young Billy pulled the bradawl from his belt. His clammy hand slapped the slow-moving hull. "I should do to you . . ." His face sank once beneath the surface, his sodden clothes seemed to weigh like lead. "I should do to you as I did to the Turk . . ." He sank a second time and his fist rapped on the moving hull. ". . . but that I love my friends, your crew!" And so saying, he rolled over in the sea, face-down. The bradawl fell away, away out of his hand, down to where the whale bones lie.

Ragged Emperor

A CHINESE LEGEND

IF ALL CHILDREN took after their parents, Yu Shin would have been a wicked, feckless boy. His father was a flint-cold man who thought with his fists, except when he was plotting some new torment for his son. Yu Shin was often lucky to escape with his life.

But Yu Shin was nothing like his father, nor even like his mother, who lifted not a finger to help her poor boy, and let him work like a slave around the farm. "Fetch the water! Feed the animals! Clean the stables! Weed the ground!"

Yu Shin did it all, and with good grace, too, as though his parents were the dearest in the world, and the work his favourite pastime. Inwardly, though, he was sometimes crushed with weariness and misery at the thought of being so unloved.

In truth, his favourite pastime was to read and study. Whenever he could, he crept away to the schoolmaster's house and sat at his feet, listening to any and everything the wise man said. "Always remember, Yu Shin," said the teacher, "not all men are like your father. Whenever things look black, have courage and pray. Life will not always be this hard."

Not always be this hard? No. It got harder. Yu Shin's father dimly perceived that his son was becoming more intelligent than he; that bred in him a kind of fear. And when Yu Shin grew tall, strong and handsome, his father grew even more afraid. Soon he would not dare to beat and kick and bully the boy, just in case Yu Shin should hit him back. No, the boy must be got rid of.

"Yu Shin! It is time for you to make your own way in the world. Out of my great generosity, I'm going to give you the Black Field, to live on and grow fat. There! What do you say?"

Now the Black Field was a patch of ground the old man had won playing mah-jong. It was miles away in the shadow of mountains, and having been to look it over, he had come home disgusted, telling his wife, "It's nothing but wilderness. I was robbed."

Yu Shin knew all this, and his heart shrank at the idea of banishment to the Black Field. But he remembered the words of his teacher and bowed dutifully to his father. "I am grateful for your tender care and for this most generous gift, dear Father." His father gave him one last kick, for old time's sake, and laughed till he split his coat.

Arriving after the long walk, Yu Shin found the Black Field even worse than he had imagined. Thorny weeds and briars choked acres of stony dirt. Here and there lay a dead tree, there and here a boulder big enough to shatter a plough. Not that Yu Shin had a plough - only his bare hands to work the worthless plot. A ramshackle hut no bigger than a tool shed slumped in one corner of the field, empty of furniture and full of draughts.

Yu Shin took a deep breath. "Oh gods and fairies, you have watched over me till now, watch over me here, too, that I may not die of starvation or despair." Then he bent his weary back, and began to pick up stones, throwing them aside, trying to expose some little piece of soil to plant.

As he worked, he happened to look up and see a distant dust cloud moving towards him. As it came closer, he could make out large grey shapes. *"Elephants?"*

Not just elephants, but a flock of magpies too, escorting the herd like black-and-white fish over a school of whales.

Yu Shin felt oddly unafraid. Even his malicious father could not have organized a stampede of elephants to trample him. So he stood his ground, and the elephants lumbered straight up to him, streaming past to either side. Flank to flank, trunks waving, they stationed themselves about the Black Field, wrenching up tree stumps, pushing aside boulders. Under their gigantic feet, the smaller stones crumbled to dust. The magpies swooped and darted in between, uprooting weeds and thistles and slugs, fluttering under the very feet of the elephants, perching to rest on their great swaying backs.

"Oh thank you, beasts! Thank you so much!" cried Yu Shin, scrambling to the top of a heap of stones to survey his land afresh. The soil was black and crumbly now, rich with elephant manure and just waiting for a crop. "Let me fetch you water! Rest now, please! You're working yourselves too hard!"

But until the elephants had finished their work, they neither ate nor rested. Then they formed a line in front of Yu Shin and dropped on to their front knees, in a respectful bow, just as if he were someone who mattered! The magpies circled three times round his head before flying away - a black-and-white banner streaming over an army of marching elephants.

They were no sooner gone than more visitors came into sight. Narrowing his eyes against the low sun, Yu Shin saw nine young men walking ahead of a rider - a girl with a cloak of shining hair reaching almost to her tiny feet. At the gate of the Black Field, the nine bowed low. "Your field needs planting, sir, and your crops will need tending. Grant us the honour of working for you."

"Oh but where could you sleep? How would I pay you? How could I feed you until my crop is grown?" Yu Shin cast a desperate glance behind him at the ramshackle hut no bigger than a tool shed. And lo and behold! It was all mended! Big rain clouds were coiling over the mountaintop, and he begged his visitors to hurry inside before the downpour began. But as he opened the door for them, Yu Shin stopped short.

"What do you see, sir?" asked the young men.

"One would think, by your face, sir, that you saw an elephant in your living-room," whispered the girl.

"No. No elephants," whispered Yu Shin.

But there *was* room enough for eleven to sit down and dine, and afterwards to lie down and sleep. The inside of the hut had become as huge as a mansion, and along a trestle table lay a feast for eleven, just waiting to be eaten.

Yu Shin did not sit down at the head of the table: he sat the girl there. He did not serve himself until everyone had filled their bowls. He did not

bore his guests with talk of elephants and magpies, but asked politely about their journey and what books they had read lately. And, of course, they talked about farming.

But to the girl he barely spoke. His rank was too humble for him ever to speak of love to such an elegant beauty. Even so, when he looked at her, it was the only topic which sprang to mind. "I would welcome your help," he told them, "but as friends not farmhands. For you can't possibly be of lower rank in the world than I am!" and he laughed, so that all his guests laughed too.

Every day, out in the Black Field, Yu Shin worked as hard as anyone. Within the year, the whole province was talking of the Black Field - not just of its record harvests, but of the oddly happy little community which farmed it.

The rumours reached Yu Shin's home. "Curse the boy," said his father, grinding his teeth. "He's done it all to spite me!"

The rumours reached the Emperor, far away in the Imperial City. "Send for Yu Shin!" said the Emperor, and that is a summons no man can refuse.

Yu Shin had no idea why he had been summoned. His ten friends offered to keep him company, which was heartening, but when, after twelve days of walking, the white spires of the Imperial City came into sight, Yu Shin trembled from head to foot. "Oh gods and fairies, my dear teacher told me always to have courage. Lend me some now, for mine is almost used up!"

The girl came and put her hand on his sleeve. "You have done nothing wrong, Yu Shin, therefore you have nothing to fear from the Emperor. Have courage a little while longer." And it seemed to Yu Shin that she knew something that he did not.

"YU SHIN!" bellowed the court usher. "BOW LOW BEFORE THE EMPEROR OF CHINA!" Yu Shin's nose was already pressed to the imperial floor. High on the Dragon Throne, clothed in gold, the Emperor clapped his frail, pale hands. "Listen, Yu Shin! Hear me, people of the Imperial Court! The eyes and ears of the Emperor are everywhere. For many years now my spies have brought strange news from the borders of my empire:

of a boy who was meek and obedient to his parents, uncomplaining and brave, who was born wise, but had the greater wisdom to listen to others. I was curious. So I sent my nine sons and my only daughter, to see if the stories were true, to see if this paragon truly existed. They tell me that this same boy is also just, generous and courteous, that all people are equal in his eyes, and all are his friends. I am old now, and my strength is failing. I mean to step down from the Dragon Throne. That is why, Yu Shin, I have sent for you. To take my place." Yu Shin lifted his nose off the floor, eyes round with wonder. "My daughter looks on you with love. Marry her. Then if you rule China as you have farmed the Black Field, China will flourish as never before!"

History does not record what Yu Shin's father said when he heard the news. Oh, history says that Yu Shin's rule was a golden blaze of achievement, but rarely mentions that he was a farmer's son, for who would ever dream a peasant boy could become the Emperor of China?

History does not mention, either, what became of Yu Shin's father. But those elephants must have dumped their trunkfuls of tree stumps somewhere, then settled down. Those magpies must have dropped their beakfuls of weeds and thistles somewhere, then roosted.

Uphill Struggle

A GREEK LEGEND

YOU CAN defy the gods just so often: they will always have the last word. The Immortals, you see, have time on their side. They only have to wait, and the disrespectful will be brought to their knees by old age and the fear of dying.

Sisyphus, though, feared nothing. He did not give a fig for their trailing clouds of glory, for their thunderbolts or lightning. In fact, as he said more than once, he thought they were a bunch of rogues and that living at the top of a mountain must have affected their brains, for they were all as mad as bats.

When Zeus, King of gods, mightiest of the mighty, stole the wife of River Alopus, Sisyphus went and told Alopus straight out - just like that. "It was Zeus, the philandering old devil. He's got your wife. I saw him take her."

78

That was too much for Zeus, King of gods, mightiest of the mighty. *"Death! Go and tell Sisyphus his time has come!"* he spluttered, as the jealous husband swirled round his ankles, set urns and couches afloat, and rendered heaven awash with mud.

Sisyphus took to his heels and ran. Death lunged at him with a sickle, but Sisyphus ducked. Death tried to fell him with a club, but Sisyphus jumped just in time. Death loosed avalanches and wild animals, but Sisyphus bolted for home and slammed the door, jamming it shut with furniture.

"I can't hold him off for long," he told his wife. "So listen. When I'm dead, I want you to throw my body in the rubbish pit and have a party."

"Oh but dearest . . . !"

The door burst open and, with a gust of wind and a crash of furniture, Sisyphus fell dead, his soul snatched away to the Underworld to an eternity of dark: silenced by the gods.

"He has *what?!*"

"A complaint. He wishes to complain, your lordship."

Hades leaned forward out of his throne, eyes bulging, and his herald cowered in terror. *"Just who does he think he is?!"*

"A poor benighted soul, shamefully and shoddily treated," said Sisyphus, entering without permission and stretching himself out face-down before the Ruler of the Dead. "I complain not of dying, Lord Hades. Far from it! It's a privilege to share the dwelling place of yourself and so many eminent ghosts! But my wife! My wretched wife! Do you know what she has done?"

Hades was intrigued. "What has she done?"

"Nothing!" cried Sisyphus leaping up and clenching his gauzy fists in protest. "No funeral rites! No pennies on my eyelids. Not a tear shed! She simply dumped my body in the rubbish pit! She's a disgrace to the very word 'widow'!"

Hades nodded his infernal head slowly, so that his piles of pitchy hair stirred within his chair. "The rubbish pit. That's bad. She shall be punished when she too dies."

"No need, my lord! Don't trouble yourself! Only send me back there, and I shall make an example of her that will teach the Living a lesson in caring for the Dead!"

"SEND YOU BACK?" Hades was stunned by the boldness of the suggestion. "Would you come straight back afterwards?"

"The moment she's been taught a lesson, I promise," said Sisyphus. Hades hesitated. "Do you know, lord? She never even laid a tribute on *your* altar in remembrance of me!"

"*Then go back and teach her the meaning of respect!*" cried Hades, leaping up in his excitement. *Appalling woman!*

"Excelling woman," said Sisyphus kissing his wife tenderly.

"I did right?"

"You did perfectly. Here I am to prove it - first man ever to escape the Underworld!" He shook vegetable peelings out of his hair, having only just recovered his body from the rubbish pit. He had promised to return to Dis, Land of the Dead, by midnight. But by midnight he would be fishing on the seashore, by morning dozing among the lemon groves, the sun on his back. Sisyphus felt so full of life that he could have palmed Mount Olympus and thrown it out to sea like a discus! "They haven't the wit they were born with!" he told his wife. "And I, Sisyphus, have the wit to outwit them from now till the revolution! One day soon, humankind will rise up and rout the gods as they routed the Titans before them. I'm *never* going back!"

When Sisyphus did not return to Dis as promised, Hades loosed his hounds on the scent. Black as tar, they came panting out of the earth, tongues lolling over bared teeth. From their Olympian palaces the gods watched, smirking, as the dogs closed on their prey, submerged him in their pitchy pelts and dragged him down to Dis.

"Such nerve! Such daring!" said Hades towering over his prize. "I am so impressed, I mean to do a deal with you, my audacious friend. You see that hill, and that boulder? Simply push that boulder to the top of the hill, and you shall go free, leave here, live for ever, *go home.*"

And so Sisyphus pushes his boulder up the hill. He has been doing it now for four thousand years. His hands bleed, his back is twisted and bent. Every time he gets to within one push of the top, the gods on Olympus swell their cheeks and - *pouf* - the boulder rolls thundering down to the bottom. He must begin again.

Nearby, Tantalus, condemned for his crimes to a pool of fire, never able to taste the sweet cool water placed just out of reach, looks up and takes his only scrap of comfort in an eternity of torment. "At least I am not Sisyphus," he tells himself, "rolling his rock for ever and a day."

But Sisyphus, as he slides down the rocky slope on his bare feet, and sets his shoulder to the stone for the millionth time, says, "One day soon Man will rise up against the gods, and then . . . and then!"

Sun's Son

A MYTH FROM TONGA

> "Who's your father? Can't you say?
> Where's your father? Gone away?"

OVER AND OVER the other children chanted it, until Tau burst into tears and ran home to his mother. "Who is my father? I must have a father! Tell me who he is!"

His mother dried his tears. "Take no notice. Your father loves us both dearly, even though he can't live with us, here."

"Why? Why can't he? Is he dead?" His mother only laughed at that. "Who *is* he? You must tell me! I have a right to know!" On and on Tau nagged until at last his mother gave in and whispered in his ear, "You are the son of the Sun, my boy. He saw me on the beach one day, loved me, shone on me, and you were born."

She should never have told him. Tau's eyes lit up with an inner sunlight, and he bared his teeth in a savage grin. "I always knew I was better than those other boys. I never liked them, common little worms. Well, now I've done with them. Now I'll go and find my father and see what *he* has in mind for me!"

His mother wept and pleaded with him, but Tau considered himself too splendid now to listen. Pushing a canoe into the sea, he paddled towards the horizon and the Sun's rising place. "Tell your father I still love him!" his mother called.

As the Sun came up, Tau shouted into his face, *"Father!"*

"Who calls me that?"

"I! Tau! Your son! I've come to find you and be with you!"

"You can't live with me, child! My travelling has no end. I have always to light the islands and the oceans!"

"Then at least stay and talk to me now!" called Tau.

And the Sun was so moved to see his human son, that he actually drew the clouds round him and paused for a brief time over the drifting canoe. "I suppose you will become a great chief on Tongatabu when you grow up," said the Sun proudly.

"Stay on Tongatabu?" sneered Tau. "Among all those common people? Not me! I want to ride the sky with you each day!"

"I regret, you cannot," said the Sun. "But you are lucky. There's nowhere lovelier than Tongatabu and no one sweeter than your mother . . . I must go now. The world expects it of me."

"Is that all you can say?" retorted Tau resentfully. "Is that all it's worth, to be the son of the Sun?"

The Sun was rising from the ocean now, shedding his disguise of cloud, shining brighter and brighter, hurrying to make up time. "Tonight my sister the Moon will rise in the sky. She will offer you the choice of two presents. One is brotherhood, the other glory. Choose brotherhood, my son! For my sake and for your dear mother: choose brotherhood! It will make you happy!" His booming voice receded to the bronze clashing of a gong, as the Sun reached his zenith in the noon sky.

"Brotherhood, pah! He wants me to be like all those others," said Tau aloud to himself. "He wants me to forget who I really am and be mediocre, like the rest. He doesn't want me. He doesn't care one coconut about me." Full of self-pity, Tau curled up and went to sleep in the bottom of the canoe.

He was woken by a piercing white whistle which made him sit bolt upright. There in the sky, like a mother's face looming over a cradle, the Moon his aunt looked down on him. "Have you come to give me my present?" he asked rudely.

She scowled at him. "Who do you take after? It isn't your mother and it certainly isn't your father. But yes, I have a present for you. Tell me, which do you want?"

Hanging down from her horns, like the pans of a pair of scales, hung two identical packages. Neither was big and neither was recognizable for what it was. "This is glory, and this is brotherhood," said the Moon.

"Give me glory!" barked Tau.

"Think, nephew. One of these gifts will do you good, one will bring you harm. Please choose carefully!"

"I told you already!" said Tau. "I know what my father wants: he wants to forget all about me. He wants me to go back home and forget who I really am - prince of the sky! He's afraid that if I take glory I'll be greater than him - burn him out of the sky. That's what. Give me glory! Give it now!"

She reached out the other package - brotherhood - but he paddled his canoe directly into her round silver reflection on the sea's surface, and scratched it, so that in pain she let drop her other hand. Snatching the parcel called "glory", Tau hugged it to his chest.

He ripped off the wrappings and there, as beautiful as anything he had ever seen, was a seashell round and red and luminous as a setting sun. "Now I shall be a god," said Tau. "Now I shall be worshipped instead of doing the worshipping. Now everyone on Tongabatu will bow down and worship *me!*"

But first the fish came to worship Tau.

Startled by a sudden rushing noise, he looked up and saw the surface of the ocean bubbling and churning, as every fish for miles around came shoaling towards the magic of the red shell. Dolphins and flying fish leapt clean over the canoe. Sharks and tunny herded close, rubbing their sharp scales against the boat in ecstasies of adoration. The spike of a marlin holed the boat. The fluke of a whale struck the sea and showered Tau in spray. Shoals of tiny, glimmering fish sped the frail vessel along on a carpet of colour, while ray flapped darkly out of the water to trail their wings over the canoe's nose.

"No! Get away! You'll drag it under! Get off the canoe!"

But the fish were in a frenzy of worship, entranced by the glory Tau held clenched in one hand. The canoe was swamped in seconds and plummeted down from under him. And although Tau was carried along for a time, on the writhing ecstasy of the fish, as soon as the red shell slipped from his hand, they let him go, let him sink. Thanks to the shark, his body was never found: he who would have been elected Chief of Tongabatu, if only he had valued his fellow men. If only he had chosen brotherhood.

The Founding of London

A VIKING LEGEND

THE FOUR SONS of Ragnar were playing chess when the news came that their father was dead.

"Dead? The mighty Ragnar Lodbrok?" said Ivar.

"Dead? Greatest of the Vikings?" said Bjorn.

"Who killed him?" said Hvitserk.

"How, when he wore his magic shirt?" said Sigurd.

They listened in horror to how Ella, King of Northumberland, had routed the army of Ragnar, captured the noble old warrior and thrown him into a pit of snakes. "At first the snakes could not pierce the shirt, it's true," panted the messenger. "But at last Ella guessed there was magic in it and had it torn from your father's back ... Then the snakes, oh the snakes ...!" The messenger broke down and wept at the memory of it.

But Ivar had no time for tears. "Lift me on to my shield, brothers, and may the gods shut me for ever out of the halls of Valhalla if I do not destroy this Ella of Northumberland!"

"Too late! Too late!" wailed the messenger. "His army is close on my heels - his and a dozen armies besides! They outnumber us twenty to one! The glory of the Viking eagle is falling, falling!"

"My oath is sworn!" replied Ivar. "I must fight."

Ivar, crippled from birth, was lifted on to his shield. Each brother held it high on one hand while with the other he drew his brazen sword. Raised up high, Ivar wielding his archer's bow was a rallying point for the Viking warriors. He loosed arrows like rain in a storm, and every one found its mark.

But Ella's army was huge. Among his allies was King Alfred of high renown, and soon the Norsemen for all their bravery were utterly defeated. Bjorn and Hvitserk and Sigurd set their brother down at the feet of King Ella like a payment of ransom, and the haughty King spat on him.

"Do you admit defeat?"

"We do," said Ivar.

"Am I the victor?"

"You are," said Ivar. "And I swear I will never raise weapon against you, if you will grant me just one boon in your mercy."

"What is it?" snapped Ella suspiciously.

"As much of this sweet land of England as may be enclosed by the skin of an ox, a little ox."

Ella beamed magnanimously. "One ox skin? Take it. That should give you just enough ground to be buried in, ha ha!"

An ox hide was brought, and a sharp knife, too. Ivar began to cut the hide into the thinnest of strips.

"What are you doing?" said Ella uneasily.

"No more than you permitted," Ivar replied.

Thousands of strips he cut from that one ox hide. On the banks of the River Thames, Bjorn laid down the first. Hvitserk laid another end-on to it. Sigurd placed a third. End-to-end the strips were laid, along and along the green watermeadows . . . over several hills, across a bridge, round the

houses clustered by the river. By the time the last strip of skin met with the first, the sons of Ragnar had encircled thirty acres of prime land, and laid claim to the Middle Thames.

King Ella was furious, but what could he do? He had given his word. As he watched the four brothers and their defeated army build a wooden city-stronghold in the middle of his kingdom, he comforted himself that Ivar had given his word too: never to fight him again.

They called the city Lunduna Berg, which became London, in time. There Ivar Lodbrok made his home, at the heart of Ella's empire, though his brothers went back to Denmark. He did not sit idle. He did not chafe at his confinement within these wooden walls. During his childhood, while other boys played, sickly Ivar had studied the magic of the runes. Now he cast the runes all day long, and the Saxons outside his walls heard the click of these mystical stones which could foretell the future: *click, click, click.*

Every day, Ivar propped himself against the city wall and talked to the Saxons who went past. "Drink my health tonight, won't you, at the inn?" he would say and throw down a gold coin. "Please accept this small wedding gift," he would call as a wedding party danced by, and throw down his jewelled cloak clasp. "Would you care to dine with me?" he would say to the starving beggars curled up against the palisade. The music of his minstrels carried far beyond the bounds of Lunduna Berg.

Ella meanwhile ruled with cruelty and spite. He taxed the people till they groaned, he worked them till they dropped. He quarrelled with his allies, brawled with his ministers and sacked the generals in his army.

"How goes the world with you?" Ivar called down genially from his city's wooden towers.

"Worse than bad," came the reply from hungry Saxons driving skinny cattle out to plough ground as stony as Ella's heart.

"That's the trouble with kings," Ivar would murmur. "Kings take the credit for victories but never take the blame for the bad times." Little by little, he and his fellow Londoners befriended the Saxons . . . and having befriended them, stirred them up to rebellion!

"*You* should lead us! *You* should be our king," the Saxons were soon saying. But Ivar always shook his head.

"I gave my word never to fight Ella. I cannot break it."

"Listen to him! Such an honourable man!"

Ivar smiled. "*I* gave my word . . . But, of course, my brothers never did . . ." So the unhappy Saxons sent word to Denmark, begging Bjorn and Hvitserk and Sigurd to come back and save them from Ella's tyranny. When the brothers landed, everyone rallied to their eagle flag.

This time there was no King Alfred to fight at Ella's side, no alliance of nations, no army of thousands. Though Ivar kept his word and never raised a bow against him, Ella was utterly defeated. It was the enemy within which beat him - an enemy citadel built at the heart of his own kingdom, yes, but also that cruel snake-pit of a heart within his barbarous breast.

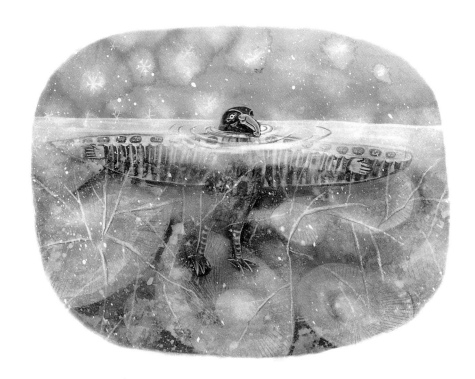

The Woman Who Left No Footprints

AN INUIT LEGEND

THEY HAD NO children, but they had each other. And so great was the love between Umiat and Alatna that they had happiness to spare for their neighbours. An old lady lived nearby with her granddaughter, and if it had not been for the kindness of Alatna and Umiat, who knows what would have become of them during the harsh winter months? As it was, Umiat caught them meat to eat and Alatna sewed them warm clothes. That little girl spent so much time playing at their house, she might as well have been their own daughter.

Then one day, Alatna disappeared. She did not get lost, for then she would have left footprints. She did not meet with a bear, for then there would have been blood. No. Her footprints went ten paces out of the door and into the snow ... then disappeared, as if Alatna had melted away.

Umiat was desolated. He beat on the door of every house, asking, "Have you seen her? Did you see who took her?" But no one had seen a thing, and though the people tried to comfort him, Umiat only roared his despair at them and stamped back home. From that day on, he did not eat, could not sleep, and if anyone spoke to him, he did not answer. Someone had taken his wife away, and he no longer trusted a soul.

Then one evening the little girl came and took him by the hand. Silently she led him to her grandmother's house and the old lady said, "You and your wife were good to us. Now it is time for us to help you."

She gave him a magic pole, an enchanted staff of wood. "Drive this into the snow tonight. Then tomorrow, go where it points. It will take you where your heart desires to be."

For the first time a flicker of hope returned to the man's sallow face, and he took the stick, stroked the little girl's hair, and went home to sleep. The stick he drove into the snowdrift by his door, and sure enough in the morning it had fallen over towards the north. Umiat's one desire was to be with his wife, so he picked up the stick, put on his snowshoes and tramped north. The old woman and the little girl stood at the village edge to wish him well. "Remember!" the old woman called. "The name of the stick is October!"

Each time Umiat rested, he stuck the stick in a snowdrift and, each time, the stick keeled over (as sticks will that are driven into snow). But Umiat trusted the old woman's advice. And after three days' journey through the wildest terrain, the stick sensed the closeness of Alatna. It pulled free of Umiat's hand and set off at a run: it was all Umiat could do to keep up with it! End over end it poled through the snowy landscape, and Umiat sweated in his fur-lined coat with running after it.

The stick led him to a valley well hidden by fir trees and hanging cornices of snow. And in the valley stood the biggest snowhouse he had ever seen, smoke coiling from the smokehole. Outside the door hung something like a huge feathery cloak.

As Umiat watched, a man came out of the hut and lifted down the garment. As he put it on and spread his arms, Umiat could see: it was a gigantic pair of wings.

So *that* was why his wife had left no footprints! This bird-man had swooped down out of the sky and snatched her away. At the thought of it, Umiat's fists closed vengefully round the magic stick. But the bird-man had already soared into the sky and away, the sun glinting on his fishing spear.

Alatna recognized her husband's footfall and ran to the door even before he knocked. "I knew you'd come! I knew you'd find me! Quick! We don't have long. Eagling will be back as soon as he has caught a walrus for supper. And he has such eyesight, from the air he could spot us for sure!"

"Then we'll wait for him," said Umiat calmly, "and buy more time." Instead of starting back for the village at once, Umiat hid inside the snowhouse.

When, with a walrus dangling from each claw, the villain landed outside the door, Alatna went out to greet him "Is that all you've brought me? Is that all you care for me? I said I was hungry! A couple of miserable walruses won't make me love you, you know! Now fetch me two whales and we shall see!"

So Eagling put on his wings again, despite his weariness, and flew out of the valley towards the sea. And while he was gone on this marathon journey, Umiat put Alatna on his back and they left the valley. Leaning on the magic stick now for support, Umiat strode out as fast as he could go.

But by the most disastrous stroke of luck, Eagling's return flight brought him swooping directly over their heads! A vast sperm whale dangled from each claw, and at the sight of his prisoner escaping, Eagling gave a great cry of rage and let his catch fall.

The impact half-buried Umiat and Alatna in snow, but they were not crushed. They scrambled over the huge flukes of the whales' tails and made for a river gorge where there were caves to hide among. Crawling into one, they lay there holding their breath, hoping Eagling would think them crushed beneath the whales.

Eagling was not so easily fooled. He saw where they had gone, knew where they were hiding, though the narrowness of the gorge prevented

him swooping on them. "You shan't escape me so easily!" he cried in his shrill, squawking voice. And plunging his huge clawed feet into the river, he spread his wings so as to dam the flow completely.

Little by little, water piled up against his broad chest and his massive wingspan, deeper and deeper, flooding the river till it burst its banks, till the gorge began to fill up like a trough.

"Oh my dear Umiat, I'm sorry!" cried Alatna. "You should never have tried to rescue me! Now look! I've brought death and disaster on both of us!" They held each other tight and tried to remember the happiness of their time together in the village. They thought of the little girl next door and so of the old lady who had lent Umiat the running stick . . .

"And its name is October!" cried Umiat, remembering all of a sudden the old woman's last words to him.

Just as the floodwater lapped in at the mouth of the cave, into its menacing, swirling depths, Umiat threw the magic stick with a cry of, "October!"

In the second that it hit the river, the stick brought to it the month of October – that very day, that very moment in October when the rivers slow and gel throughout the arctic wilderness; when they slow and gel and fleck with silver, thicken and curdle and freeze.

Eagling, submerged up to his chin in the rising river, wings outstretched, was trapped in the freezing water as surely as a fly in amber. Umiat and Alatna stepped out on to the ice and crossed gingerly to the other side, pausing only to pull one feather defiantly from the bird-man's head.

Within the day, they came in sight of the village. And there the old lady and the little girl stood, waiting and waving.

"I'm sorry! I have lost your magic stick, Grandma!" Umiat called as soon as they were close enough to be heard.

"But you have found your heart's desire, I see," she replied. Then, watching Alatna and the little girl hug and kiss and laugh for joy, she said, "I think we've all found our heart's desire today!"

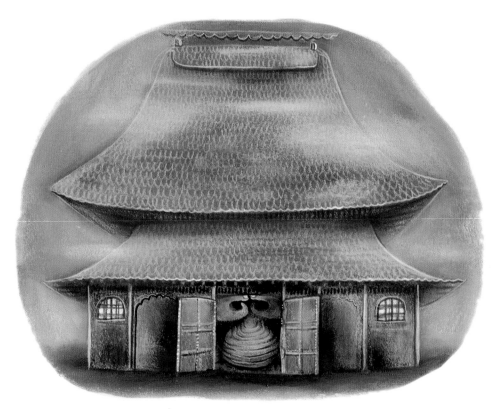

Biggest

A JAPANESE LEGEND

WHEN THE PEOPLE of Kamakura decided to cast a statue of the Buddha, their love for him was so enormous that the finished masterpiece was the biggest in the world. Cast in gleaming bronze, it caught the sun's light like the burnished waves of the evening sea - until, that is, a temple was built to house it, a temple rising almost to the sky. The statue towered over the people who had made it, and they were full of wonder, for they were sure they had never cast the look of calm and kindness on the huge bronze face. News spread through the whole world that the Buddha of Kamakura was the biggest, the loveliest, the most wonderful thing under the heavens.

When word reached the Whale, the Whale said, "Nonsense!" It shook so hard with scornful laughter that waves slopped against fifteen shores.

97

But on every one of those shores, fishermen mending their nets were busy talking to each other about the wonder at Kamakura: "... It's the biggest, the loveliest, the most wonderful thing under the heavens, you know ..."

"But *I* am the biggest, the loveliest, the most wonderful creature under the heavens," said the vain creature. "That's how I know these stories cannot be true!"

Still, the rumours played on his mind, until he could bear it no longer. With a whistle, he summoned his friend the Shark and asked him, "Can there be any truth in these stories?"

"I'll find out," said the Shark, and swam to the shore of the ocean at Kamakura. From the water's edge she could see the new temple rising almost to the sky. "That must house the Buddha," she thought. "Big! But how big! And how can I find out? I can't swim up the beach or swing from tree to tree."

Just as she was about to give up, a small rat came scuttling by with a fishhead in its jaws. "Sir! Would you do me the very great favour of going up to that temple over there and measuring the statue inside it?"

"The Buddha?" said the rat. "Certainly! It's always a pleasure to go there. It is the biggest, loveliest, most marvellous thing under the heavens, you know." Away trotted the rat, up the hill, in under the temple door, and round the base of the statue.

Five thousand paces! The Shark shook and shivered at the sheer sound of the words. Five thousand paces? What would the Whale say?

"Five thousand paces? From where to where? From nose to tail? From stem to stern? Whose paces, and how long is their stride? Believe the word of a rat? Never!" That was what the Whale said.

But though he tried to ignore the news, he could not put it out of his mind.

"There's nothing for it," he said at last. "I'll just have to go and see this pipsqueak for myself."

And so he took down from the Continental Shelf his magical boots, and put them on.

The tides rose high that night. Rivers flowed upstream, waves broke with such a surge that seaweed was left hanging in the trees. Moonlit meadows were flooded with saltwater, when the Whale waded ashore that night, in his magic boots. Dripping and glistening, he rolled his blubbery way up the hill and slapped with one fin on the great carved temple doors.

The priests were all sleeping, so no one heard him knock. No one, that is, but the Buddha, dully luminous in the candlelit dark. The candle flames trembled, as a voice like distant thunder said, *"Come in!"*

"I can't come in," said the Whale. "I am too vast, too huge, too magnificent to cram myself into this little kennel!"

"Very well, then, I shall come out," said the Buddha mildly, and by bending very low, he was just able to squeeze through the temple doors. As he straightened up again, the Whale blinked his tiny eyes with shock. The Buddha, too, stared with wonder at the sight of a Whale in magic boots.

The noise of the temple gongs vibrating woke a priest. Glancing towards the Buddha's bronze pedestal he saw, to his horror, that the statue,

the precious wonderful, adored statue, was gone! Had thieves come in the night? Had the Buddha sickened of so many curious visitors? The priest ran shouting out of the temple. "Help! Quick! The Buddha is . . . is . . ."

There, eclipsing the moon, stood two gigantic figures, deep in conversation amid a strong fishy smell.

"The very person we need!" said the Buddha, spotting the priest. "Perhaps you would be so kind, sir, as to settle a small query for this excellent cetacean? Could you please measure us both?"

The priest fumbled about him for something, anything he could use for measuring. Untying his belt, he used that. One . . . two . . . three . . . scribbling his measurements in the soft ground with a stick.

When he had finished, the priest fretted and fluttered, he stuttered and stammered: "I sincerely regret . . . I'm dreadfully sorry . . . I can't lie, you see, I have to tell the truth, your divinity . . . but the Whale is two inches bigger than you."

"Knew it!" The Whale whirled round in his magic boots, shaking the ground, setting all the temple bells jangling in the breeze he made as he blew out triumphantly through his blow-hole. "I knew it! I knew I was the biggest, grandest, most marvellous creature beneath the heavens! Never doubted it for a moment!" And away he strode, leaving a smell of fish in the air and large, deep bootprints in the ground.

"Oh master, are you very distressed?" the priest asked of the statue. "We could fetch more bronze and make your feet thicker, your forehead higher!"

The Buddha smiled a peaceable smile, utterly unconcerned by the night's events. "It means nothing to me and much to him that he should be the biggest. Think nothing of it. I am very content to be as I am. Please don't lose another moment's sleep over it."

The priest mopped his brow and crept back inside the temple. A handful of peaceful words followed him, fragrant with the scent of the blossoms outside.

"Besides . . . the Whale has still to take off his boots."

"I Love You, Prime Minister!"

A FRENCH LEGEND

THE EMPEROR Charlemagne conquered the world ... then was conquered himself by a woman. He fell in love with Princess Frastrada from the easternmost regions of his vast Empire, and such was his passion for her, his adoration, that Prime Minister Turpin always suspected some magic at the bottom of it.

Frastrada was beautiful, gentle and good, but was she so far above every other woman, that Charlemagne the Mighty gazed at her all day long, could not bear to be apart from her, took her on every campaign, and invited her to every conference of state? Turpin had his doubts.

When Frastrada died, he was certain. Somehow she had cast a spell over Charlemagne, and the magic did not even end with her death. Now the Emperor sat by her body, rocking and groaning, cradling Frastrada in his arms and wetting her cold face with his tears. All government was forgotten, all affairs of state let go. He would not eat or drink, nor leave the room where her body lay; would not permit the Princess to be buried.

The Prime Minister could not let this unhealthy state of affairs go on. So when at last the distracted Emperor fell asleep across the bed, exhausted with crying, Turpin tiptoed in and began to search. He did not know what he was looking for - what charm, what amulet, what magic hieroglyph - but he searched all the same, until just before dawn, he glimpsed something in the dead Princess's mouth.

Poor Frastrada. Her love for Charlemagne had been so desperate, that she had begged her eastern men of magic for a charm: something which would ensure her all-powerful husband never tired of her. They forged her a magic ring. Growing ill, realizing she was about to die, Frastrada looked at the ring on her hand and wondered what would become of it. Would another woman wear it and be loved by Charlemagne as much as Frastrada had been loved? No! The thought was unbearable. So, in the hope of remaining the one true love of Charlemagne's life, she slipped the ring into her mouth just as Death stole her last breath.

"Who's there? Frastrada? What - " Charlemagne was stirring.

Turpin, sooner than be found robbing the dead Empress, slipped the ring on to his own finger just as his master sat up, fuddled with sleep. Charlemagne opened his eyes and saw his . . .

"Dearest Prime Minister!"

"Good morning, my lord."

"How wonderful to see you! I'd forgotten how very handsome you are. What, hasn't this woman been buried yet? How remiss. Oh, Prime Minister! Oh dear, *dear* Prime Minister, may I just say what a comfort it is, at a time like this, to have a man like you by me I can rely on." And flinging both arms round Turpin, Charlemagne dragged him away to breakfast.

Inwardly Turpin crowed with delight. He had saved the Emperor from dying of grief, and therefore saved the Empire from crumbling into chaos. Besides, all Turpin's advice would now sound as sweet as poetry in Charlemagne's ears. He got permission for his favourite roadbuilding schemes, he got laws passed, he got posts at the palace for all his friends and relations . . . not to mention the presents - horses, chariots, a few small countries . . . All because he was wearing the magic ring.

Even so, after a time Turpin began to wish that perhaps the ring were not *quite* so powerful. Just when he wanted some peace and quiet, the Emperor always wanted to talk, to hold hands, to listen to music with his dear Prime Minister. On campaign, Turpin had to sleep in the Emperor's tent. And the generals in the army, the princes, the kings of minor provinces gave him very odd looks as Charlemagne stroked his hair and bounced Turpin on his knee. Turpin's wife was put out, as well.

In fact, Turpin began to be extremely sorry he had ever put on the ring. But how could he be rid of it? Give it to someone else? No! That someone would be ruling the Empire before long, whispering new policies in the Emperor's ear and being given all the privileges of a . . . well . . . a prime minister.

Could he bury it? What if Charlemagne became rooted to the spot

where the ring was buried, fell passionately in love with a garden bed or half a metre of desert sand? What if Turpin were to drop it in the sea? Would Charlemagne hurl himself into a watery grave?

Turpin examined the ring with utmost care. Around the inside was engraved an inscription: "From the moon came my magic; in the moon my magic ends." Had the ring fallen from the moon, then? Oh no! How could a mere prime minister return it there? Night after night, Turpin walked sleepless around palace or camp, turning the problem over in his mind.

One moony night, when the imperial army was camped in a forest, Turpin crept from the Emperor's tent, desperate for a little solitude. He wandered among the trees, a broken man. He simply could not stomach one more poem composed to the beauty of his nose, one more statue of him raised in a public place, one more candlelit supper where Charlemagne gazed at him - "How I love you, Prime Minister!" - all through the meal. Enough was enough. Turpin resolved to run away.

But just then, he found himself beside a lake. It was large and smooth, with a reflection of the moon floating at its heart. Impetuously Turpin pulled off the ring. A little smudge of gold flew over the water. A small splash at the centre of the moon's reflection set ripples spreading. The ring was gone for ever.

Dawn came up while Turpin walked back to the Emperor's tent. As he lifted the flap, the sunlight fell across Charlemagne's face and roused him.

"Yes, Turpin?" said the great man, raising himself on one elbow. "*Must* you bring me problems of state quite so early in the morning? What is it?"

Turpin bowed low respectfully and backed out, letting the tentflap fall. "Nothing, my lord. Nothing that cannot wait."

Outside, Turpin gave a little skip and a hop. The spell was broken. He was a free man, a happy man - apart from the explaining he had to do to his wife.

The army struck camp, the Emperor mounted up, and a thousand banners fluttered on their way through the forest. Within the hour, they came to the lake. "Stop!" cried Charlemagne. Turpin chewed anxiously on his glove. The Emperor gazed about him, one hand over his heart, smiling open-mouthed with wonder. "I've never seen anywhere like it! What do you say, Turpin? Isn't this the loveliest spot you ever saw?"

"Magical, my lord."

His knights and courtiers looked about him, puzzled. Pretty, yes, but a tree is a tree and a lake is a lake. But Charlemagne, not realizing that the drowned ring was still working its magic, found the forest clearing too ravishingly beautiful for words. He could not tear himself away. All day long he strolled its shores, picked flowers from its banks.

"I shall build a palace here, my greatest palace, my home. One day, when the world is all mine, I'll live here, I'll be happy here. If only Frastrada could have seen this place ..."

True to his word, Charlemagne did build a palace in the forest, beside the lake, and whenever war and politics permitted, he lived there. A little town grew up around the palace - Aix-la-Chapelle it was called - and wherever Charlemagne travelled, however far afield, he never could quite put Aix from his mind. No more than he could ever quite forget his dear dead wife, Frastrada.

And the Rains Came Tumbling Down

A MYTH FROM PAPUA NEW GUINEA

"WHAT WE NEED are houses," said Kikori.

"What's one of those?" said Fly (since houses had not yet been invented).

"Somewhere to shelter from wind and sun and rain - other than this cave, I mean, with its spiders."

Fly pretended to be unimpressed, but liked the idea. Kikori suggested they build a house together, but Fly had ideas of his own about building the very first house and he was sure they were the best.

Kikori built a wood frame, then wove the leaves of the rei plant into five glossy waterproof mats: one for a roof and four for the walls. It was laborious, painful work. The sharp leaves cut his hands and irritated his skin, but the finished house was so fine that his family broke into spontaneous clapping.

Not Fly. He had long since finished his house and returned to watch, with much shaking of his head and carping. "How long you took! Look at your hands. Makes me itch just to think. And it's *green*. Do you seriously think people want to live in green houses?"

"How did you make yours, then?" said Kikori patiently.

Kikori examined Fly's house, his head on one side then on the other. Fly's framework of branches had been daubed all over with mud. The mud had dried into clay, and now the hut crouched on the ground like a collapsed beast, boney with protruding sticks.

"What happens when it rains?" said Kikori.

At that moment, a clap of thunder sent them both darting back to their huts, mustering their wives and children. The monsoon broke as if the green sky had split, and the rains came, as they come every year to Papua New Guinea. Every view was lost from sight behind a curtain of rain. Every sound was silenced by the deafening hiss of the downpour.

Inside Kikori's house, he and his family sat listening to the thunderous rattle of water on rei. But the interwoven leaves threw off the rain as surely as a tortoise's shell, and they stayed warm and dry. They sang songs and planned which crops to plant in the sodden earth.

Fly, too, sat with his family inside his new house. The rain ran down its brown sides, and gradually the clay walls turned back to mud around them. The mud oozed and trickled. It slopped down like cow pats on to Fly and his wife and children, smothering them from head to foot in brown slurry.

But not for long. Soon so much icy rain was pouring through the roof that they were washed quite clean again. The children's teeth chattered, his wife moaned gently to herself, ground her teeth and wrung out her hair. When the rain slackened briefly, she went out with a panga and cut a great pile of rei leaves, dropping them down at the door.

"When you've made a house like Kikori's," she said, "I and the little ones will come and share it with you. In the meantime, we're going back to the cave."

Fly, as he sat ankle-deep in mud, contemplated the unfairness of life and whether he ought to invent dry rain.

The Golem

A JEWISH LEGEND

IN THE COURSE of any day, there are dull, repetitive jobs to be done. The more intelligent the man, the more wearisome routine seems to him. So that when the rabbi, Judah Loew ben Bezabel, contemplated the daily round of cleaning, bell-ringing, winding of clocks, checking of candles, mending of vestments, it seemed to him that no man (or even woman) should waste his God-given life doing it. So he built a creature - without mind, without soul, with little shape and no family - to do all the tedious tasks within the Prague synagogue. He called it the Golem, which means "lifeless lump of earth". Under its tongue, Judah put a tablet, and the tablet empowered the limbs to move, the shapeless trunk to heave itself about.

It was hideous to look at, but who would see it? The Golem went about his work in the gloomy unlit synagogue when no rabbi or worshipper was present. It pulled the candle stubs from their sconces and fetched new ones, polished the brass and swept the floor, muttered meaningless words from no living language, as it sewed the vestments, washed the windows and scared cats off the front steps.

Perhaps Judah should have written GOLEM on his creature's forehead. But as it was, he wrote the word he loved best: AMETH, which means truth. Once, when old Mordecai the grocer accidentally caught sight of the creature scrubbing amid the shadows, he gave a cry of, "Oh! Death has come for me!"

Judah sent the Golem away, and laughed, and soothed the old man's fright. "It's not Death. That's only my Golem."

"But he has 'Death' written on his forehead!"

"No, no. Not METH, but AMETH," said Judah, and smiled at the mistake. "The 'A' was hidden in the shadows, you see?"

Through his dull, glintless years, the Golem looked out on a world of stone and brass and wood. Sometimes he heard singing and liked that. Sometimes the sun shone through the coloured window-glass and splashed over the Golem like a shower of gems. His last sight each night was of

Rabbi Judah's face, large near his own, fingers reaching into the Golem's mouth to remove the tablet. Then darkness closed over him like a coffin lid.

But one day, Judah Loew ben Bezabel forgot to remove the tablet. (He was an intelligent man, and such routine little jobs tended to slip his mind.) The Golem moved on around the empty hall of the synagogue, though all his tasks for the day had been done. He went to check the steps, but there were no cats. The night street stretched away like a dark corridor, so naturally, he began to sweep it.

The broom wore down to a stump. Dawn came up, and the sun shone full in the Golem's face for the first time.

He went mad with joy.

It was the ferocious joy of the Earth as it shakes down trees and houses. It was the destructive joy of a young child who knows no better than to break things. When people saw the Golem on the streets, they screamed, "A monster! A ghoul!" and he did not like that. He hurled the people through windows, for the joy of seeing the glass shatter. He hurled carts into the river, for the sake of the splash. The tablet under his tongue suffused his body with more strength than ever before, his rudimentary mind with new thoughts. He must taste more of this new, brighter world!

But the light hurt his eyes, the screams hurt his ears, and he could not find his master. People were throwing things at him now, and firing loud guns. The Golem began dimly to feel pain and fright and rage. He tore the walls out of buildings, looking for Judah. He climbed church spires and threw down clocks and gargoyles. Though they tried to kill him, no one could, because he was never truly alive - a lump of clay.

But then God made Man out of a lump of clay, and Judah had made something very like.

When the statues would not speak to him, the Golem pushed them down. The colourful market stalls intrigued him: he snatched down the awnings. The army got in his way, and so he shooed the soldiers away, like the cats from the synagogue steps.

But where was Judah? The cacophany of a city in panic maddened and amazed the Golem, and he ripped off doors and punched down fences, looking for his master, calling for him in a shapeless language nobody understood.

He was hurt. He was lost. By the time Judah Loew ben Bezabel came running, robes flapping, face aghast, the Golem blamed *him* for the dazzled turmoil of his mind. He left tearing up horse-troughs, and turned on Judah with a grotesque snarl. His shapeless hands closed round the rabbi's throat, and they both fell to the ground.

Judah, half-throttled, saw the world shrink to a dim, half-lit confusion. His strength was puny in comparison with the Golem; he knew he could never fight it off. But with his last conscious thought, Judah reached up and struck the Golem's forehead - smudged out the letter "A" from the word *ameth:* left the word *meth: death.*

The Golem's eyelids flew open; the eyes beneath were not dim, but flashing bright. *"Life, not Death!"* he said, quite plainly, then fell forward with the weight of a horse on top of Rabbi Judah.

I ought to mention: the Golem was only tiny, only waist-high to a real man. You may see for yourself. What remains of the Golem stands in a glass case in Prague Museum, a clay figurine as ugly as sin, the Hebrew for "Death" still scrawled on his forehead.

The Hunting of Death

A MYTH FROM RWANDA

AT THE START, God thought the world of his people: their smiles, their dancing, their songs. He did not wish them any harm in the world. So when he looked down and saw something scaly and scuttling darting from nook to cranny, he gave a great shout.

"People of Earth, look out! There goes Death! He will steal your heartbeat if you let him! Drive him out into the open, where my angels can kill him!" And fifty thousand angels flew down, with spears, clubs, drums and nets, to hunt down Death.

All through the world they beat their skin drums, driving Death ahead of them like the last rat in a cornfield. Death tried to hide in a bird's nest at the top of a tree; he tried to burrow in the ground. But the birds said, "Away! God warned us of you!" And the animals said, "Shoo! Be off with you!"

Closer and closer came the army of angel hunters. Their beating drums drove Death out of the brambles and tangles, out of the trees and the shadows of the trees, on to the sunny plain. There he came, panicked and panting, to a village.

He scratched at doors, tapped at windows, trying to get out of the glare of the sun, trying to get in and hide. But the people drove him away with brooms. "Go away, you nasty thing! God warned us about you!"

The angel huntsmen were close on his heels when Death came to a field, where an old lady was digging.

"Oh glorious, lovely creature!" panted Death. "I have run many miles across this hard world, but never have I seen such a beauty as you! Surely my eyes were made for looking at you. Let me sit here on the ground and gaze at you!"

The old lady giggled. "Ooooh! What a flatterer you are, little crinkly one!"

"Not at all! I'd talk to your father at once and ask to marry you, but a pack of hunters is hard on my heels!"

"I know, I heard God say," said the old woman. "You must be that Death he talked of."

"But *you* wouldn't like me to be killed, would you - a woman of your sweet nature and gentle heart? A maiden as lovely as you would never wish harm on a poor defenceless creature!" The drum beats came closer and closer.

The old woman simpered. "Oh well. Best come on in under here," she said and lifted her skirt, showing a pair of knobbly knee-caps. In out of the sunlight scuttled Death, and twined himself, thin and sinuous, round her legs.

The angel huntsmen came combing the land, the line of them stretching from one horizon to the other. "Have you seen Death pass this way?"

"Not I," answered the old lady, and they passed on, searching the corn ricks, burning the long grass, peering down the wells. Of course, they found no trace of Death.

Out he came from under her skirts, and away he ran without a backward

glance. The old woman threw a rock after him, and howled, "Come back! Stop that rascal, God! Don't let him get away! He said he'd marry me!"

But God was angry. "You sheltered Death from me when I hunted him. Now I shan't shelter you from him when he comes hunting for your heartbeat!" And with that he recalled his angel huntsmen to Heaven.

And since then no angel has ever lifted her skirts to hide one of us, not one, until Death has passed by, hunting heartbeats.

The Monster with Emerald Teeth

A MAYAN MYTH

EVEN THE GODS make mistakes. First they populated the world by carving little wooden men and women. But the carvings were so badly behaved that their very belongings rose up against them. Their knives stabbed them, their chickens pecked them, their houses fell on them, their millstones ground them to splinters.

But the giants who replaced the wood-men were no better. Vukub-Cakix and his two sons, Earth-Mover and Earth-Shaker, were proud, vain and cruel. Even after the gods had produced their masterpiece - humankind - the three giants made life a misery for everyone on earth. They had to be got rid of. But how?

The heavenly twins, Hun-Apu and Xbalanque were sent to rid the earth of the three giants, and went at once to the nanze-tree where

Vukub-Cakix picked fruit each day. Hiding in the branches, they waited till Vukub had climbed right to the top of the tree before levelling their blowpipes and taking aim.

"Owowo!" cried the giant, and fell, clutching his face. Though he crashed to the ground like a meteorite, the fall did not kill him. Indeed, now he could see strangers in his fruit tree, he came after them, silver eyes flashing, grinding his emerald teeth. He grabbed Hun-Apu's arm and pulled it clean off before the heavenly twins were able to make their getaway.

"I need it back!" said Hun-Apu when they stopped running. "I can't go back to Heaven without my arm!"

"Don't worry," said Xbalanque. "But now our friend the giant has the most fearful toothache. Our darts hit him in the mouth."

"I'm not feeling too good myself," said his twin.

But they put on cloaks and masks and went to the house of Vukub-Cakix, where the giantess Chimalmat was just roasting Hun-Apu's arm for dinner.

Terrible groans came from the bedroom, for the giant was in agony. "I'd just reached the top of the tree," he told his wife, "when this terrible toothache started up. If it hadn't been for that, I'd've have brought you home both those thieves to eat."

The twins knocked at the door:

"We were just passing . . . couldn't help hearing . . . wondered if we could help . . ." they told Chimalmat, ". . . we being dentists."

She hurried them in to where Vukub lay writhing on his bed, swearing horribly and promising to make the world pay for his misery. Green lights flickered over the ceiling as the firelight reflected off Vukub's emerald teeth.

"Say 'aaah'," said Hun-Apu.

"Mmm. Just as I thought. All rotten. Those teeth will have to go," said Xbalanque, peering into the cavernous mouth.

"But all his power is in his teeth!" whispered Chimalmat in awed tones. "All his strength! How will he bite off his enemies' heads? How will he grind their bones?"

"We shall give him a new set, of course," said Xbalanque and began, with pliers, to pull out the emerald teeth one by one. A whole emerald

mine never held so many jewels as Vukub-Cakix's mouth.

In place of the emeralds, Hun-Apu and Xbalanque left grains of maize. No more did the green fire flicker on the ceiling, no more did Vukub's silver eyes shine. He faded, faded, faded, like a fire going out. Powerless to lift a finger, he watched the darkness close in on him like a rising flood and carry his soul away.

"What about my arm!" said Hun-Apu when the twins got outside. Xbalanque threw back his cloak and brandished the limb he had rescued from over Chimalmat's fire. "A little magic," he said, "and you'll be as good as new." And so he was.

Earth-Shaker was a braggart and a show-off. That made him easy to flatter and easier still to find. When the heavenly twins tracked him down, he was busy juggling three small mountains.

"Stupendous!" exclaimed the brothers, bursting into applause. "So clever! Such strength!"

Earth-Shaker looked down at them, pleased. "Yeah. There's no mountain I can't move. Name one, any one. I'll show you. Nothing's beyond me."

Xbalanque pointed to a distant snowcapped peak. "That one?"

"Easy," bragged the giant.

"It must make you hungry, all this pushing and juggling," suggested Hun-Apu. "Perhaps we could shoot you something to eat?"

Earth-Shaker liked that idea. He was always hungry, always devouring the wildlife tenderly placed by the gods, in the woodlands and hills. As a flock of macaw flew over, the twins put their blowpipes to their lips and brought down a pair of birds. Then smothering them in mud and baking them over a fire, they presented the meal reverently to Earth-Shaker. They did not mention that the darts in their blowpipes were poisoned with curare, that the mud they had used was poisonous, too. By the time Earth-Shaker had eaten his meal, his head was spinning and his silver eyes were dim. He could barely even see the mountain he was supposed to move.

Xbalanque and Hun-Apu led him there, ignoring his whimpers, saying that he was trying to worm out of a challenge. "He can't do it, you see, brother? He was just bragging," they said.

So Earth-Shaker, in his insane pride, pushed against the mountain till his sweat ran down it in rivers. He pushed so hard that he left hand prints, a fathom deep. But then his heart burst with the strain of so much poison and so much showing off.

Which left only Earth-Mover, proudest giant of them all.

He was nosy by nature. So the heavenly twins dug a pit which looked like the foundations of an enormous house, and waited. When Earth-Mover came along, he at once climbed down to inspect the pit, thinking what a big house must be planned and how he might just take it for himself.

He saw the huge pile of timber logs stacked beside the hole, but he did not realize, until too late, that Xbalanque and Hun-Apu stood behind the logs with crowbars, levering them forward.

One by ten by hundreds, the huge tree trunks tipped, rolled and fell into the pit on top of Earth-Mover. They fell with the noise of an avalanche, and when the noise stopped, all was silent.

"Come one, come all and build on the ruins of the Giants!" declared Xbalanque. "Build a fine home for yourselves over the broken bones of Earth-Mover; you and your families will be safe now from his bullying!"

The young men did just that. Four hundred of them built a log house big enough for all of them to live in, and when it was built, they had a party to celebrate.

But beneath them, Earth-Mover was not dead at all. He had found himself a crevice safe from the falling logs, and there he had bided his time, silver eyes gleaming, grinding his emerald teeth. At midnight he got to his feet, flinging up his head, flinging out his arms, tossing the house and its four hundred occupants into the night sky. It was like the eruption of a volcano.

So high were the young men thrown, so wide their eyes with terror, that Xbalanque looked up and saw the moonlight glimmer in eight hundred eyes. And in that instant, he transformed the boys into stars, to keep them from falling to their deaths.

Heartsick and angry, the heavenly twins worked alone to avenge the young men. They undermined two mountains towering over a deep ravine and, when Earth-Mover walked through the ravine, Xbalanque toppled one mountain on top of him and Hun-Apu toppled the other.

Like a blanket, the rocks and earth rucked and folded over the fallen giant. This time he must surely die! But out between the boulders reached a hand, grasping, clawing. Out through the solid earth burst another. And so Xbalanque and Hun-Apu invoked the magic of the heavens, the magic of the gods which had made the giants a thousand years before.

And Earth-Mover was turned to stone, petrified, stopped stock-still and lifeless in the very act of grasping for life.

The Boy Who Lived for a Million Years

A ROMANY LEGEND

THERE WAS once a boy - the son of the Red King - who had the ambition to live for ever and never to grow old. So he said to his father, "Give me a horse and my inheritance, and I shall travel the world till I find what I am seeking."

Now the Red King was rich, and Peter's inheritance came to six sacks of ducats - far too much to carry. So he carved a treasure chest out of rock, and buried it with his treasure inside, under the city wall, marking the place with a cross. "I shall come back for this when I've found the place where I can live for ever and never grow old."

Over and under and into and out travelled the Red Prince Peter, for eight years, until he came to a continent called Forest, all covered in trees. In the forest grew an oak tree. And enthroned in the tree sat the Queen of

Birds - not an owl or an eagle but a green woodpecker.

"What do you seek in my dappled kingdom, young man?" she asked.

"A place to build my castle where I shall live for ever and never grow old."

"Then build here," said the Queen, "for I and my friends shan't die till I have pecked away the last twig of the last branch of the last tree in this forest."

"In that case, you will die one day," said Peter, "and this is not the place for me."

He travelled along and throughout, wherever and however the lanes took him, for eight years more. And he came at last to a palace of copper set amid seven mountains, each one a different colour of the rainbow. Inside the gleaming copper palace lived a Princess more beautiful than any in all the undulating world. On her walls were written, a million times, the name "Peter", and in her picture frames hung nothing but portraits of him.

"In my mind's eye I have seen you, and I have loved you ever so long, Prince Peterkin," she said.

Now many men would have ended their search for happiness then and there, but Prince Peter was utterly single-minded. "I shall stay in no place with no woman unless she and I can live for ever and never grow old."

"Then you were meant for me!" exclaimed the Princess, flinging her arms round his neck. "For those who live in the Copper Castle shan't grow old or die till the wind and rain have worn the seven mountains flat."

Red Peter wriggled free and pushed her roughly away. "Then that day will surely come. I've seen the rain and I've heard the wind, and this place is not for me."

On and away, farther than far, the Red Prince travelled for eight years more, until he came to a pair of mountains, Gold and Silver, and nearby, the lair of the Wind. To Peter's surprise, the Wind, for all his fame and strength, appeared to be only about ten years old.

"I have searched the world over for a place where I can live for ever and never grow old," said Peter to the Wind. "You roam far and wide; tell me where I can find such a place."

"You have found it," said the Wind.

"Until?"

The Wind looked puzzled. "You spoke of 'always' and 'never'," he said, "and so did I. Stay if you will, and go if you care to, but here you will never grow old or die."

Red Prince Peter crowed with delight, and accepted the Wind's invitation. There was fruit enough in the trees and colour enough in the sunsets to satisfy any man. There was water enough in the streams and time enough for everything.

"Only take one piece of advice," said the Wind. "Hunt on Golden Mountain; hunt on Silver Mountain. But don't go hunting in the Valley of Regret or you will be sorry you did."

The mountains of Silver and Gold had game enough to satisfy any hunter. For a hundred years Prince Peter hunted there, and hankered after nothing, not even the beautiful Princess in her palace of copper. Not one hair of his head turned grey, not one joint in his body grew stiff, and it seemed to him that no more than a week had passed. Even his horse remained young.

Then one day in one of the many centuries, found Peter chasing a deer. The deer leapt over branch and log, over river and ditch, off the Mountain of Gold and into more shadowy groves, damper and darker and *deeper*

down. Realizing he must have strayed into the Valley of Regret, Peter immediately turned back. But all the way home he had the strangest feeling of being followed - a feeling he could not shake off.

Into his heart crept a small wish: to see his home again. Later it grew to a longing, later still, a burning ambition. After a while, he missed his home so much that he was sorry he had ever left his father's city.

"I'm leaving now," he told the Wind, who shrugged.

"Tell me something I didn't already know," said the Wind.

On his way home, Prince Peter passed the place where the seven mountains had stood. Through the teeming rain, all he could see was the copper palace, green with verdigris, overlooking a flat and dismal plain. As he passed by the window of the Princess, the rain washed away the last stony grain of the last mountain, and the palace buckled and fell with a clashing crash. The Princess reached out a withered hand towards the Red Prince, and cursed him as she fell.

Eight years later, Prince Peter passed across the continent called Forest, but all that remained of the forest was a single twig held in the claw of a green woodpecker. The woodpecker, Queen of the Birds, drilled to sawdust that last twig of the last branch of the last tree, then fluttering into the air, fell dead at Peter's feet.

He did not pause to bury her, but galloped on towards home, the city of the Red King, his father. But when he reached the place … there was no city, hardly one brick on another, and not a living soul he knew. "Where is the city of the Red King?" he demanded of an old man.

The old man laughed. "That's only a legend, sir. Never really existed. Or if it did, 'twas in a time before history books were wrote."

"Nonsense. The Red King is my father, you fool!" said the Prince. "His city stood here - a city of five thousand souls - not thirty years since! Did it burn? Was it sacked?"

The old man closed one eye and sniffed. "Were you born mad, sir, or did it come upon you sudden?"

Exasperated, Prince Peter dragged the old man to the spot where his treasure lay buried - six sacks of ducats, under the castle wall. "I'll prove it to you!" he declared.

Breaking open the ground, he dug out the stone chest and, with his sword, prised it open, breaking the blade as he did so. The lid fell back with a dusty crash. "There! What did I tell you? Six sacks of ducats!"

"Yes, sir, but you did not speak of the other."

Peter looked again. To either side of the six sacks sat two old crones, one dark, one fair.

"My name is Old Age," said the dark-haired one, taking Peter's wrist in a bony hand.

"My name is Death," said the fair, grasping his other wrist.

And that is where Prince Peter, son of the Red King, met his death after a million years of life.

So I'll wish you happiness and long life - but not so long as a million years, for that, in my opinion, would be a kind of a curse, rather than a blessing.

About the Stories

All these stories have been passed down from generation to
generation by word of mouth and changed a little by each successive story-
teller, growing and altering to suit the listener. I have retold them - sometimes
from the briefest passing reference in dusty old volumes -
to please you, the reader.
In doing so, I have made sometimes small, sometimes large changes, but have
tried to preserve an inkling of the pleasure each story gave to its original audience.

G. McC.

About the Stories

Sadko and the Tsar of the Sea   *14*

The *byliny*, epic poems of old Russia, tell of a race of demi-gods, ancient champions, *bogatyri*. Massively strong, amazingly brave, capable of magic, they were nevertheless Christian heroes. One, transformed into stone, is still to be seen in Kiev Cathedral which he supposedly built.

Cupid and Psyche   *20*

Here is the remarkable ancestor of a fairy tale now popular the world over. *East o' the Sun, West o' the Moon* is easily recognizable in this Roman myth. It may have been first set down in writing by Apuleius, in the second century AD, in his book *The Golden Ass*. Since Psyche means "soul" and Cupid represents physical love, the story is also about the two elements at work in true love.

The Armchair Traveller   *26*

Ganesa is the Hindu god most honoured by poets and writers. His likeness – a pot-bellied, four-armed, elephant-headed dwarf demon - is found in many houses in India, and offerings of fruit and vegetables are made to him.

Doctor Faust   *31*

Georgius Sabellious lived in sixteenth-century Germany: a doctor, fortune-teller, astrologer and magician. He roused the anger of the Church, but had several rich and influential clients. After his death, the rumours about him were wild and inventive. "Faustus Junior" (as he called himself) became the subject of fairground puppet shows.

Alone   *35*

The Native Americans of the North-West Pacific coast tell this story of a time before the region was populated. It is extraordinary not only for its wistful melancholy, but also for the picture of a primeval world devoid of men, heroic or otherwise.

Bobbi Bobbi!   *37*

Most Australian myths are set during the Alchera or "Dreamtime". This story, told by aboriginal Australians in the north, is one of them.

THE GINGERBREAD BABY *41*

Many familiar stories begin with a woman unhappy because she cannot have children. In Arab Palestine, it is a particularly common theme, and childlessness is portrayed as the one fault no husband can forgive. Originally, this old lady made seven helpful trips abroad while waiting for her bread to rise.

THE PRICE OF FIRE *45*

Every culture has a myth to explain how fire fell into mortal hands. Mostly the fire is stolen from God at great peril, and someone has to suffer for it, as in this tribal myth from Gabon in West Africa.

SEA CHASE *49*

The *Kalevala* is Finland's epic myth cycle and this story only one episode from the huge enthralling saga. Lapland is an ethnic region straddling the northlands of Finland, Sweden and Russia.

YOUNG BUDDHA *58*

Two and a half thousand years ago, in the city of Kapilavastu, a prince was born to the King of Shakyas. According to legend, until the age of twenty-nine he lived a life of blissful luxury, then gave it all up to seek perfect wisdom and a solution to suffering and death. It took him six years of trial and error. After his enlightenment he taught the "Middle Way" which is at the foundation of Buddhist thinking, not just in India but all over the world.

THE BATTLE OF THE DRUMS *63*

The Mandan tribe of native North Americans live on the plains, dependent on the buffalo herds for food and shelter. Lone Man is their "founding father" and protector, this story the origin of their ritual chants, dance and drumming.

THE GOLDEN VANITY *68*

This story is usually sung as a ballad. There are many versions, the oldest of which names the treacherous Captain as Sir Walter Raleigh, no less, and the ship as his vessel *Sweet Trinity.*

RAGGED EMPEROR *71*

Magic plays a great part in Chinese legend, and though Yu Shin's story is a moral tale of virtue rewarded, it is also just as much of a fairy story as *Snow White*. In longer versions, Yu Shin's guardian fairy repeatedly saves his life in fantastical ways, as his father tries to kill him.

UPHILL-STRUGGLE *78*

In Greek mythology, Sisyphus is the grandfather of Bellerophon, another thorn in the side of the gods. For Bellerophon, even more ambitious than his grandfather, tried to reach the halls of Olympus, flying upwards on his winged horse.

SUN'S SON *82*

Tonga, loveliest of the Polynesian islands, gave rise to this story of pride. Properly speaking, the boy's choice is between Melaia and Monuia, abstract magical words ·not easily translated.

THE FOUNDING OF LONDON *87*

The founding of London is one small incident in the thirteenth-century saga of Ragnar Lodbrok (or Ragnar Leather-Trousers). In it England figures simply as one overseas colony among all the others which the Danesmen conquered.

THE WOMAN WHO LEFT NO FOOTPRINTS *92*

The Inuit tribes of Alaska set this story in the village of Na-ki-a-ki-a-mute during the month of Naz-re-rak-sek, or October. This is surely an indication of the myth's significance: a celebration of the coming of the winter freeze, when rivers mystically turn to solid ice.

BIGGEST *97*

Japanese merchants measure soft goods, such as material, with one yardstick, and solid goods, such as metal, with another. The soft "whale yard" is five centimetres longer than the other – surely the origin of this legend . . . unless the legend is the origin of the difference. Castastrophic storms have destroyed much of Kamakura, including the temple, but the huge Buddha still stands.

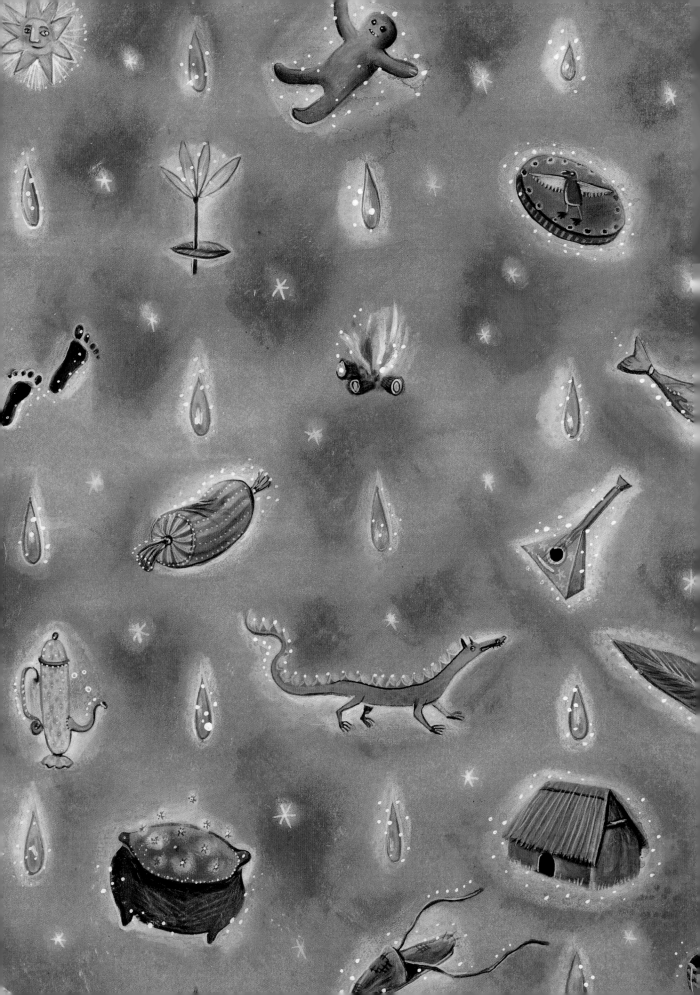